"Look, I would *know* if I were dead," Noh began. "I can promise you that—"

The boy interrupted her. "I've seen it happen before. Lots of times. No one really wants to be dead. They're scared of it."

He extended a hand toward Noh.

"I'm Henry."

"Noh. Short for Noleen."

She reached out a hand to shake Henry's but found, to her utter amazement, that her hand slid right through his.

"Oh, goodness!" Noh exclaimed. "You really are dead."

# AMONG THE GHOSTS

## BY AMBER BENSON
### ILLUSTRATED BY SINA GRACE

## Aladdin
NEW YORK   LONDON   TORONTO   SYDNEY

This book is a work of fiction. Any references to historical events, real people, or real locales are used fictitiously. Other names, characters, places, and incidents are the product of the author's imagination, and any resemblance to actual events or locales or persons, living or dead, is entirely coincidental.

**ALADDIN**

An imprint of Simon & Schuster Children's Publishing Division
1230 Avenue of the Americas, New York, NY 10020
First Aladdin paperback edition September 2011
Text copyright © 2010 by Amber Benson
Illustrations copyright © 2010 by Sina Grace
All rights reserved, including the right of reproduction in whole or in part in any form.
ALADDIN is a trademark of Simon & Schuster, Inc., and related logo is a registered trademark of Simon & Schuster, Inc.
Also available in an Aladdin hardcover edition.
For information about special discounts for bulk purchases, please contact Simon & Schuster Special Sales at 1-866-506-1949 or business@simonandschuster.com.
The Simon & Schuster Speakers Bureau can bring authors to your live event. For more information or to book an event contact the Simon & Schuster Speakers Bureau at 1-866-248-3049 or visit our website at www.simonspeakers.com.
Designed by Lisa Vega
The text of this book was set in Bembo.
The illustrations for this book were rendered digitally.
Manufactured in the United States of America / 0811 OFF
10 9 8 7 6 5 4 3 2 1
The Library of Congress has cataloged the hardcover edition as follows:
Benson, Amber.
Among the ghosts / Amber Benson. — 1st Aladdin hardcover ed.
p. cm.
Summary: While spending the summer at The New Newbridge Academy, where she will soon begin sixth grade, Noleen finds strange things happening and discovers the special talent her aunts saw in her when she was a motherless infant.
ISBN 978-1-4169-9405-3 (hc)
[1. Ghosts—Fiction. 2. Boarding schools—Fiction. 3. Schools—Fiction. 4. Aunts—Fiction.
5. Supernatural—Fiction. 6. Mystery and detective stories.] I. Title.
PZ7.B447158Amo 2011
[Fic]—dc22
2009029392
ISBN 978-1-4169-9426-8 (pbk)
ISBN 978-1-4424-0940-8 (eBook)

For all the "realies" out there who know
that ghosts do indeed exist

## Acknowledgments

I want to thank my editor, Liesa Abrams, for helping me make Noh's story as good as it could possibly be.

# Contents

# Ants and Sweaters

Thomas spied the ants as he waited by the back door to the kitchen. At first he ignored their merry procession, his mind overwhelmed with thoughts of the rich, buttery apple pie that he knew was baking in the oven only a few feet from where he was standing. Once or twice he let his eyes flick away from the window in the kitchen door in order to mark the ants' progression, but it was only *after* he saw Mrs. Marble pull the golden-crusted beauty from the oven that he gave the ants a real looking at.

From what Thomas could tell, it seemed like the ants were on their way home from a military reconnaissance mission in the kitchen. They marched single file down the concrete steps that led to the kitchen door, across the sidewalk, and into the grass. They each carried a small piece of white fluff on their backs, which to Thomas made them all look like they were wearing little angora sweaters. A grin splitting his face at the thought of ants in knitted sweaters, he decided that the white stuff was definitely *not* angora, but something edible that the ants had stolen from Mrs. Marble's kitchen.

Thomas didn't like anyone stealing from Mrs. Marble—even the ants. Mrs. Marble was the nicest lady in the whole world as far as Thomas was concerned, besides which she baked some of the best pies this side of the Mason–Dixon Line . . . or at least, that's what everyone said after they'd sampled one of her delicious desserts.

Feeling like a police detective in search of a crime—a policeman was something Thomas had always wanted to be when he grew up, after being a chef, of course—he decided to follow the ants and see where they were going. He pushed his brown newsboy cap out of his eyes and followed the thieving insects across the school grounds, past the archery field, and back over to the burned-out shell of the West Wing.

There had been a fire in the West Wing a number

of years before, and now most people kept away from the building. Thomas thought those people were silly for being scared of an old, burned-out building, but he guessed that anyone was allowed to feel any way they wanted to about stuff that scared them. Though personally he believed that *just* because something didn't look perfect anymore, didn't mean you had to be scared of it. Sometimes a pie didn't come out looking perfect, but that didn't mean you threw it away—misshapen pie tasted just as good as any other kind of pie, thank you very much!

On the steps that led into the main entrance of the West Wing, Thomas paused to tip his cap to a girl who was sitting on the topmost step. She had her nose pressed firmly into a book, but she looked up and gave him a quick grin as he passed her by. Thomas spent most of his time in the kitchen, which was where he'd worked . . . *before*, but because of this, he didn't really know the other kids at the school very well. He wasn't sure what this particular girl's name was, but he thought it began with the letter *N*—although he couldn't *really* be sure. He was much better at remembering recipes than names.

Before the grin had even left her face, the girl was

3

back into her book. Thomas saw that she didn't even notice the ants that were marching up the steps beside her. If *he'd* been the one sitting by an army of ants, he'd sure have noticed them.

Thomas went through the door that led into the interior of the building, his eyes trained on the ants' progress. Instantly he saw that the line of ants was making its way across the room before disappearing down into a small hole that sat right underneath the hearth of a large brick fireplace. Thomas got as close to the hole as he could, putting his eyeball right up to it, but it was so dark that he really couldn't see where the ants were going at all.

Suddenly Thomas felt his whole body go stiff as a strange, prickly sensation swept across him. The hairs on the back of his neck stood up at attention. Thomas hadn't felt anything like this in so long that at first he almost didn't recognize what it was.

It was only when his teeth started to chatter that he realized what was happening to him. For the first time in more than eighty years, Thomas was *cold*. He looked up from where he was crouching by the base of the fireplace, and his eyes went wide when he saw what was waiting for him.

He opened his mouth to shout, but only a deep gurgle of fear popped out. It filled the empty room like the hollow sound of the last piece of candy rattling around inside a trick-or-treater's Halloween grab bag.

When the girl with the book came back inside from her perch on the stairs, the room was empty. She scratched a bug bite on her arm and looked around curiously. She was pretty sure that she'd seen the boy from the kitchen come in here only a few minutes before.

She wondered where he'd gone.

# In the Beginning

Two minutes after Mabel Maypother gave birth, she looked down into her newborn's steel gray eyes and smiled. Then she lay back on the hospital gurney and died.

Thus began the auspicious life of Noleen-Anne Harris Morgan Maypother, the wee babe clutched tightly in her dead mother's slowly cooling embrace.

Harold Maypother was distraught. Mabel had been the love of his life. He had no idea what he was going to do without her. While he quietly began to lose his grip on reality, his two sisters—and only living relatives—took possession of Noleen-Anne.

Clara was the oldest Maypother and very bossy. She had bossed Harold around from the time he was in diapers all the way up until his marriage to Mabel Harris three years earlier. Aunt Clara thought it was her job to boss. It made her happy and kept the people around her from being messy. And, in truth, by picking up where she had left off on her brother's wedding day, she probably saved his sanity that awful night.

With baby Noleen tucked into the folds of her coat, Aunt Clara marched herself and her two siblings back to Harold's small apartment and, after giving baby Noleen a bottle, sent everyone off to bed with the adage that "things always look better in the morning."

Baby Noleen woke up to find herself wrapped in a pair of warm, strong arms. She trained her gray eyes up into the smiling face of her aunt Sarah. At the time, Sarah was only sixteen, but there was something ancient in her lovely face. When she was older and better read, Noh surmised that Aunt Sarah and Florence Nightingale probably had a few things in common. But at the time, she only saw the glow that emanated from her young aunt, and it made her feel warm and loved.

"Poor little Noh," her aunt cooed. "We'll love you, motherless or not. You're a special little girl . . . even if you don't know it yet."

  8

Noh didn't understand then, but later she would. There was indeed something very special inside the little girl, something passed down through the bloodline of the Maypother women, so that in each generation there was one female child born with a special "talent." This special talent would bide its time, watching and waiting for the day when it could finally show itself—and then, whether she liked it or not, Noh's life would be changed forever.

# Noh the Magnificent

The summer had been a mess so far.

Noh was *supposed* to be spending the already messy summer with her father in the Appalachians while he studied the mating habits of the Appalachian Russell Newt. But at the last minute he had decided that his daughter was just too young to go slogging through the muck *In Search Of*, so he shipped her off to Aunt Clara's house for the summer.

When she got there—the note from her father explaining the situation clutched in her small, sweaty hand—she found that Aunt Clara had packed up her family and gone to the beach for the summer. Well, since she wasn't sure exactly what beach her aunt and cousins had decamped to, she didn't think spending the summer with them was going to be a viable solution.

Noh thought about getting back on the train and trying to find Harold, but she decided against it in the end. She thought, quite justly, that he would already be far into the woods and completely unreachable.

She sat on Aunt Clara's stoop for a good two hours, debating her options and eating the lemons (rind, seeds, and all) she had collected from the backyard.

Tired and feeling the onset of an acidy stomach, she walked back to the train station and booked a seat on the night train to New Newbridge. She knew that the only stable person in her family (i.e., guaranteed to be where they were supposed to be) was her aunt Sarah, who taught English literature at the New Newbridge Academy. And anyway, Noh was going to be starting there in the fall for sixth grade, so she figured it was as good a decision as she could make at the time.

She slept the whole way on the train. Her mind was filled with very lucid dreams that tickled her brain. She saw a boy her own age sitting at a tall desk, reading a crumpled and smudged letter. Sensing her presence, he glared angrily at her.

The old lady sitting beside her nudged her awake at the New Newbridge stop. Noh collected her bag and stepped out into a very humid summer day.

# In the Cemetery

New Newbridge was not a big town. Noh was able to navigate her way from the train station to the school without much difficulty. She had visited her aunt Sarah three times since she had taken the teaching position there three years before.

Noh's sense of "what was where" was more highly developed than if she had never been there at all, so she only got lost once—when she tried to take a shortcut through the old cemetery.

The cemetery had been in business since the pioneer days. There were graves that had been so exposed to the elements that you could barely read the rudimentary inscriptions. Noh, who was strangely drawn to any and every cemetery she had had the good fortune to come

across, clapped her hands happily and opened the creaky iron gate. Pieces of rust came off onto her hands, staining them. But she didn't mind.

No one but Noh knew why she loved cemeteries. And if you had asked her, Noh probably wouldn't have told you, anyway. But, suffice it to say, it had something to do with the word *serenity*. Serenity oozed from the graves and made Noh feel safe and secure. She imagined that when she lay in the grass near a welcoming headstone, it was like being wrapped in her dead mother's warm embrace.

It was a phantom pain she felt—being motherless. Because how could her feelings of grief be real if she had never even known the person she had lost in the first place? But still . . . it felt pretty real to her, anyway.

Noh had once tried to explain all this to her cousin Jordy, but he had only run and told Aunt Clara, who had promptly told Noh's father, who had sent her to see a psychologist in a drab gray building downtown. So, from that day forth, she had decided to keep any strange leanings to herself.

Noh walked through the old cemetery, picking wildflowers and reading the inscriptions on the headstones.

She was so intent on what she was doing that she didn't notice that she was back where she had started. The only thing that made her realize she was going in circles was that the headstone inscriptions started repeating themselves.

The next go-around, she paid more attention to where she was going. Yet when she thought she was on the other side of the cemetery, she found herself instead back at the rusty gate. It didn't matter where she started or how slow or fast she walked—Noh just couldn't seem to get to the other side. Finally, she chalked it all up to hunger and low blood sugar and slunk back out the same gate she had happily walked through two hours before.

"What're you doing here, girl? You don't belong here!"

The voice was harsh, tinged with age, and pretty mean-sounding to boot. Noh looked up, startled to find an old woman standing just inside the gate of the cemetery, glaring at her.

Noh may have been lost in thought as she had exited the cemetery only moments ago, but she wasn't blind— Noh knew the old woman hadn't been there before.

"I thought anyone could visit a cemetery," Noh said

defiantly. Usually she was pretty respectful of people older than herself, but there was something about this old woman that made her want to talk back. Maybe it was the cruel turn of the old woman's mouth or the hateful glint in her eye, but it was all Noh could do not to stick out her tongue at her.

"Don't you sass me, girl," the old woman hissed, her bony shoulders shaking beneath the homemade black woolen dress that covered her stick-figure frame. Noh couldn't help thinking that the old woman looked just like a witch. All she needed was a broomstick, a pointy black hat, and a cat.

"It's a free country," Noh said, trying not to be too rude, even though it was very hard not to say what was on her mind. "Anyone should be able to pay their respects, ma'am."

The old woman spit on the ground in front of the cemetery gate.

"This is private property," she hissed again before slamming the gate shut right in front of Noh's face. "We don't want any of your respects—we like it just as it is. We don't need *your* kind coming in and stirring things up!"

The old woman took a small stone from her pocket and threw it through the bars of the cemetery gate, where it landed right at Noh's feet. Noh reached down to pick it up, curious to find a hand-carved eye cut into its polished gray surface.

She knew exactly what this stone was . . . it was an *evil eye*.

Noh looked up, opening her mouth to protest the strange gift, but closed it when she saw that the old woman was gone. She had somehow disappeared among the graves while Noh was picking up the stone. Noh walked over to the cemetery gate and looked inside, but she could find neither hide nor hair of the crazy old woman.

She knew that the old woman probably hadn't meant the stone to be a gift, but that's exactly what Noh decided it was. She wasn't scared of the evil eye—in fact, she kind of liked it. She put it into her pocket, rubbing her fingers against its polished surface. It would be a good reminder that there was always something strange and interesting lurking *just* around the corner.

# The New Newbridge Academy

After her strange run-in at the cemetery, Noh spent the rest of her walk to the New Newbridge Academy deep in thought, trying to figure out how an old woman could simply disappear like that.

That was why she smelled the New Newbridge Academy before she saw it. The cook, Mrs. Marble, was known throughout five counties for her apple pie, and she was in baking heaven today. Noh's mouth began to water the minute the school's front drive came into view.

All in all, the school was really a hodgepodge of different architectural styles. The old building itself was Gothic with large pointed windows and ornamental gargoyles sitting benignly at the front entrance and hanging from the roof.

The architect who had designed the building had thought the gargoyles would be sufficiently scary enough to keep even the most daring students from spending too much time climbing around up on the roof.

The inside of the building was voluminous, with two floors of classrooms and another floor for administration purposes. The basement had a therapeutic indoor swimming pool that lay dormant most of the time underneath a mechanized roll-out gym floor. When there was a really mean game of basketball going on down in the gym, you could actually hear the scuff of tennis shoes on wood up in the biology labs.

Except for the basement, all the floors were made from slabs of thick gray stone that in the winter made the place as cold as a mausoleum, even when the furnace was turned way up. Between the drab gray walls, the rough-hewn stone floors, and the school crest and Arthurian-themed tapestries hanging here and there, the place had quite an imposing air. Most sixth graders spent their first semester darting through the halls in mortal fear of ghosts and goblins grabbing them on their way to English class.

  22

To her surprise, Noh saw her aunt sitting on the front steps of the main building, holding a crochet hook.

"Aunt Sarah?" she started inquiringly, but her aunt didn't let her finish. Putting down her hook and yarn, she said, "I went to the station, but I missed you by ten minutes."

"But—," she started, yet once again was stymied by her aunt's honeyed voice.

"Clara's neighbors called when they saw someone lurking about the house. I assured them that it was only an errant niece."

"But—"

Her aunt smiled. "How did I know it was you?"

Noh nodded.

"Because of the harried telegram I got from your father, telling me to go and collect you at Clara's for the start of the school year. I almost borrowed a car to come get you myself, but then the neighbors called and I knew that you were too smart to stick around until Clara got back."

"I didn't want to stay with her, anyway, but my dad said I had to." Noh's eyes filled with tears of exhaustion and hunger. Her aunt smiled and held out her arms.

  23

Noh happily rushed into the proffered hug. For the next few minutes the tears streamed down her face as she recounted her homeless adventure in only slightly exaggerated detail. When she was finally done, she handed her aunt the polished stone from her pocket.

"I think it's an evil eye, don't you?" Noh asked excitedly. She really hoped her aunt would agree. Her aunt turned the polished stone over and over in her hand, deep in thought.

"Maybe you should let me keep this," her aunt said finally, but Noh shook her head.

"It doesn't scare me. I'll just hold on to it for luck," Noh said firmly, taking the stone back and slipping it into her pocket again. Her aunt gave her a funny grin but didn't argue with her. Instead she stood up and took Noh's hand.

"Let's go get my brave girl something to eat." She smiled as she took Noh's bag and led her into the building toward the wonderful smell of newly baked apple pie.

# So, She Fancies Herself a Pioneer, Does She?

Noh settled herself into her new room with contented sighs of happiness. The South Wing, which housed all the girls, had been built to look like a villa on the Côte d'Azur. In a very forward-thinking moment the trustees had hired a woman—one of the few women architects in the state—to design the building.

Millicent Farley had grown up in Europe and had been obsessed with the southern coasts of Italy, France, and Spain. When given the commission at New Newbridge, she had been quoted as saying, "I would like to give all the young women of the New Newbridge Academy a taste of what it is like to live in paradise."

It was said that on quiet spring evenings you could

actually hear the roll of the surf from anywhere you happened to be standing in the South Wing. And the smell of suntan oil and cassis was almost palpable every day of the week.

Noh's own small dorm room was warm and cozy. The small twin bed was made up with soft cream-colored sheets and a bright geometric-patterned quilt that her aunt Sarah had made with her own two hands. The floor was smooth vanilla pine and covered with a pink and mauve woven rug. The walls were bare cream, the paint new and unchipped.

All in all, Noh was pleased. It wasn't as nice as her room back home, but it would more than do. She was sure that she could learn to live without her TV and computer. Well, pretty sure.

After a quick nap Noh decided to explore her new surroundings. Her visits to the school in the past had been no more than cursory. She had never had the opportunity to really check the place out. She figured that there was no time like the present to remedy that.

Her room was down the hall from her aunt Sarah's. Since her aunt was one of the dorm supervisors, she lived on the same hall as the youngest girls.

But when Noh got to her aunt's room, she found the door shut and locked. She knocked twice with the back of her fist, but only succeeded in hurting her knuckles. She waited in vain for Sarah to open the door, but her aunt didn't so much as cough behind the thick oak door. Finally, Noh got bored with waiting and decided that Aunt Sarah must be out and about. She shrugged her shoulders and made a quick beeline for the exit.

Once she was outside, Noh felt much better. It wasn't that the girls' dorm gave her the creeps or anything, but Noh had just never much liked being trapped within four walls and a roof. Noh breathed in the fresh air and started to run. Her first order of business was to take a quick jog around the grounds and sort out *what* was *where*.

The wind had started to pick up, and Noh's dark brown hair whipped across her face and tried to find its way into her nose and mouth. She pulled a shiny sterling-silver barrette from her pocket and pulled her hair back into a not-so-neat ponytail.

She was glad that her hair was stick straight and super-fine. Otherwise, the thin barrette would never have held

  27

her shoulder-length hair in place. The barrette had been a present from her father on her tenth birthday, and she cherished it. Her father never said, but Noh had the distinct impression that the barrette had been her mother's.

As she walked across the grounds of New Newbridge, Noh realized that they were even more picturesque than the buildings.

The football field was huge, with bleachers all around. Everett Smithers, the coach at New Newbridge from 1920 to 1950, was considered to be, by those in the know, one of the greatest high school football coaches of that century. A number of boys, after spending four years under the coach's tutelage, went on to football glory at Notre Dame, Harvard, and Yale. Sadly, after his retirement, football at New Newbridge was never quite the same.

The archery range was beautiful. It had spawned a number of state archery champions and a few "more infamous" students responsible for a number of "unintentional" peer maimings.

The stables were well cared for. The horses were either friendly and eager to please or holy terrors that spent a lot of their time in the paddock, munching grass.

 28

Artemis Lake was wide and calm as Noh stood at its edge. Amateur rowers, swimmers, sailors, and fishermen used it in the spring, summer, and fall. In the winter it was a place to go and mope around when one was feeling depressed over an unrequited crush or bad mark on a paper. Visiting the frigid winter lake was good therapy. It reminded you that even when things looked terrible, spring was just around the corner to cheer everyone up.

Noh couldn't help marveling at just how large the New Newbridge Academy was. She had known that this was the case, but somehow she had needed to see it for herself. When she came to the football field, she climbed to the top of the bleachers and sat down for a quick rest. From her vantage point she could see the whole backside of New Newbridge. She was particularly drawn to the burned-out side of the West Wing.

Noh decided that it looked as if some hungry giant had taken a bite out of the building. The missing and blackened-out parts were in stark contrast to the rest of the building, which was still in pristine condition.

Her aunt Sarah had told her that the school trustees had known how rambunctious boys could be, so they had decided to entrust the design of the East and West

Wings to an ex–army engineer. William Atherton, a twice-decorated Great War veteran, had seen it as his duty to make the place as strong as an elephant. He had reinforced the walls so that they were fist- and foot-proof, put in the hardest woods for the floors and trim, and even put peepholes in every door to instill that little bit of army paranoia that "Big Brother" was watching.

Until the fire that destroyed the West Wing, the boys' dorms were truly thought to be indestructible.

Noh wondered when someone was going to fix the West Wing and make it habitable. Not that she minded the creepiness. In fact, it was quite the reverse—she liked the sadness that she sensed emanating from the burned-out old warhorse of a building. She wondered if maybe, somewhere in its depths, there was a kindred spirit just itching to make her acquaintance.

She left the bleachers and football field behind and found herself standing directly in front of the West Wing's back door. She hadn't meant to go there, but she was unable to make her feet go in any other direction. Out of politeness she knocked on the door and waited the obligatory ten seconds. When no one came to open the door, she opened it herself.

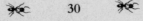

The knob was cold and hard in her hand. She didn't think that the steel would be so cold, with the weather outside as warm as it was. She closed the door softly behind her and shivered. The place was a refrigerator. Noh wished that she had brought her jacket, but how could she know that the West Wing would be a deep freeze? She thought about turning around and going back the way she had come until she could crawl into her nice, warm bed and pull the covers over her head.

But she stayed put. The place wasn't that bad, really, except for the cold.

The sunlight was still alive enough to illuminate Noh's way, so she didn't bother fumbling with the electric lights as she began to explore. Her feet made soft swooshing noises as they echoed their way across the room. Noh decided that the place she had entered must have once been the laundry room. She could almost hear the swishing of the washers and dryers.

She left that room and found herself in a long hallway that eventually dumped her out into the front entrance hall. She walked over to a large painting that hung precariously on the wall. It was placed so that it was the first thing anyone saw when they entered the West Wing from the front door.

Noh studied the drawn, grouchy face of the old man in the picture. The painting was done in oil so that the picture's subject seemed to almost glow with some inner light. *It's a shame that he has such a nasty look on his face,* Noh thought. Otherwise, it would have been a truly magnificent painting.

"He looks like he's got a bug up his butt, huh?"

Noh sucked in her breath and turned around hurriedly at the sound of the voice. The girl was wearing a yellow T-shirt and a pair of hiking boots. The book in her hand was old and dog-eared from reading.

"Yeah, he kinda does, doesn't he?" Noh responded. She had been frightened by the voice, but now was very happy to see that the voice's owner was about her own age and looked friendly.

"Do you go to school here?" the girl asked curiously. She scratched her arm as if something were biting her. Noh wondered if there were lots of mosquitoes because of the lake. Maybe she could entice her dad into visiting her by boasting about all the mosquito larvae that were to be found on the school grounds.

Noh nodded her head. "Not yet, but I *will* be going here when school starts back up again this fall." Noh watched the girl give her arm one final scratch, then leave the bite alone.

"What's your name?" The girl didn't seem to be in the least bothered by the fact that they were all alone in this creepy old building. Noh watched her carefully.

"Noh," she answered smoothly. "My name's Noh, short for Noleen."

The girl thought this was funny. She giggled.

"I'm Nelly. I'm not short for anything." The girl seemed to think that this was funny too, and laughed again.

"I should get back," Noh blurted out. "Maybe I'll see you around."

"Maybe." The girl smiled. She nodded her head up and down as if she were some kind of marionette puppet.

*Yipes,* Noh thought.

They stood in complete silence for over a minute, and then Noh broke the spell.

"Okay. Well . . . er, bye," Noh said quickly, and made a run for the front door. Finally, something—someone—was giving her the creeps.

Nelly watched the new girl run out the door. She looked down at her arm and scratched the sore spot again. It didn't really hurt. She scratched it more from habit than anything else.

She would have to tell Trina about the new girl, she thought.

Back at the girls' dormitory, Noh found the door to her aunt's room unlocked. Noh knew immediately that she should have knocked instead of just barging in, but she was unable to stop herself. Inside she found her aunt Sarah standing over a giant iron cauldron.

"You're just in time for some tea," Aunt Sarah said as she dropped a handful of rose petals into the iron pot.

# Noh, Tea in Your Coffee?

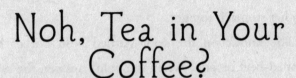

oh backed into the hallway and, without a word, walked slowly toward her room. When she got there, she opened the door and went inside. Closing the door behind her, she crawled into bed and pulled the covers over her head.

It had been that kind of day.

She stayed under the covers for a long time. She pretended that she was an embryo living in her mother's belly, growing very, very slowly. She played a breathing game in her head—every breath she took was really an echo of her mother's heartbeat.

This continued into the early evening. She finally surfaced from her make-believe world when her stomach started growling. Mrs. Marble was fixing "*something*

and chipped beef"—Noh was certain of it. There was no other smell in the whole world that compared with the smell of good old chipped beef. This made Noh feel better. At the very least, something *normal* was gonna go into her stomach tonight.

The knock on the door startled Noh out of her chipped-beef reverie. When she didn't answer, the door opened and her aunt Sarah came in carrying a tray of tea.

"I thought you might be hungry," Aunt Sarah said in a quiet voice. "Dinner won't be ready for another hour." It was as if she were trying to keep herself from saying other things instead.

"You don't have to have any if you don't want to," Aunt Sarah said even more quietly.

Noh looked down at the tray. There were two scones and a peanut butter cookie arranged elegantly around the teapot and mugs.

"Do you want to have something to eat with me?" Noh said just as quietly. Anyone looking in would have thought they were in a library. Her aunt nodded and began pouring the tea.

"When you were little, Noh, you always tried to drink my tea," Aunt Sarah said as she handed her a mug of honeyed tea. "But you wanted nothing at all to do with your father's cup of coffee."

"Oh," Noh said.

They sipped their tea in silence after that. Noh occasionally stole glances at her aunt from under her lowered eyelashes. She loved her aunt more than almost anyone else, but there was something about her aunt Sarah that—as much as it compelled Noh's love—also very much intimidated her.

"What were you doing? Before, I mean, when I barged into your room without knocking?" Noh blurted out the question, spitting bits of cookie through her lips as she talked.

"I had already had a kinda strange day, and then to see you standing over a big old cauldron like that was even stranger. . . ." Noh trailed off, unsure if she should be saying all this. But she continued on, unchecked. The words slipped from her mouth like slimy old banana slugs.

"You're not a wicked witch, are you? I mean, if you are, that's great, but it's kinda weird. If you are. A wicked witch. I mean . . ." Noh trailed off again. This was just like digging your own grave. Every inch you sank deeper into the earth just kinda creeped you out and made you feel slightly nauseated.

Her aunt put a reassuring arm on Noh's shoulder. "What if I told you that I was going to teach a history class next semester in which one would be pretending to live in the nineteenth century. Well, for the duration of each class, that is, and then one can go back to the rest of one's day living normally in the present. And the giant 'cauldron' you saw will be used to show how one did one's laundry—back before the advent of mass electrical consumption and the widespread use of modern washing machines."

Silence, as Aunt Sarah waited for Noh's response. After her own little diatribe Noh felt kind of sheepish.

"Oh," Noh said in a very teeny, tiny voice that she hoped her aunt could hear. It wasn't that she was really *that* worried about her aunt Sarah being a wicked witch. She didn't know why she had made such a big deal out of the whole thing. She supposed that it had something to do with being newly alone and feeling strange about her scholarly surroundings.

"*But* then what if that weren't really the truth? What if I really were a witch? A wicked witch, like you say.

Would that bother you, Noh?" Her aunt didn't wait for a response. She stood and patted Noh's head. "You shouldn't judge anyone on what you see with your eyes alone. And just for the record: I'm *not* a wicked witch— at least for the next semester—because I'm going to be a pioneer instead."

Her aunt closed the door on her way out, leaving Noh gape-mouthed. Noh, feeling slightly like a codfish, closed her mouth.

*Is this one of those trick-question moments?* she wondered. Was she supposed to choose one occupation or the other—wicked witch or pioneer—only to have her aunt laugh and tell her that it was just a joke? Noh thought that if it were a joke, then it was in very poor taste. But if it weren't a joke, then she'd have to make a choice, and soon, because it was almost dinnertime and she'd be seeing her aunt Sarah in the dining room over plates of chipped beef and something or other.

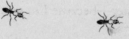

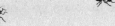

# Oh, Henry

Dust motes danced happily in the sunlight, streaming in through the two large quarter-paned windows. The dust motes were busy little creatures dancing here and there. They seemed to be having all of their summer in this one hour of sunshine.

Henry stared at them, wondering if when he wasn't there to observe them, did they dance at all? He sighed, thinking that his thoughts were getting silly.

He blinked quickly. Almost as if it were reading his thoughts, one of the dust motes seemed to be waving at him. Well, then that answered it. He *was* being silly. Dust motes didn't wave. They didn't even have arms. It had to be a trick of the light.

Henry growled at himself under his breath. Thinking about the past always made his brain go a little soft and fuzzy around the edges.

Well, what did he want? Fifty years *was* a long time to be alone. *And* memories did tend to get a bit hazy with age, so he was just going to have to learn to deal with the blurriness.

Henry reflected on this as he sat at his old, battered desk trying to reread the letters his mother had sent him while he was away at school.

His mother was a quiet woman who wrote about their farm and what she and his father had had for dinner. It was comforting in a way, but, really, it was that life that Henry had been running away from when he had left for the New Newbridge Academy.

Not that many thirteen-year-old boys were on the lam from their old lives. Well, he wasn't *really* on the lam. He was just a curious, sensitive boy who wasn't born very well suited for life on a farm. He liked getting up early to feed the chickens and hogs, but that was about it.

Actually, he got on well with the animals. He just looked into their large brown eyes and sympathized.

44

Somehow the animals knew that he understood. But feeding the animals was just a small part of what went on in the "day in the life" of a farm. It was a very visceral thing, with lots of being born and dying in a small span of time. Poor Henry got ill every time anything had to be slaughtered. These were his *friends* that his mother put on the Sunday dinner table.

But Henry wasn't reading the letters to think about all the dead, friendly animals he had eaten in the thirteen years he had been under the rule of his farm-loving parents. No, he was reading the letters because he was feeling sorry for himself. Seeing his mother's large, curly cursive writing somehow made his stomach ache just that little bit more than it already did. Henry found that feeling sorry for oneself could actually be pleasant, in a very strange way. At least once every few months he let himself sink into a dark depression and brood for a week.

Everyone knew to stay out of his way when he was in a funk. Well, everyone, that is, except for Trina. She was a real busybody who always had to have her nose in everyone else's business. When she wasn't being nosy, she was actually very nice. Henry played chess with her

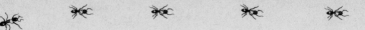

when they thought to do it. Which wasn't regularly, but almost.

Now there was a knock on his door. Henry jumped at the sound, then quickly stuffed his mother's letters back into his desk.

The door burst open and Trina came in, her face pinched with worry.

"Why are you up here skulking around like an old ninny," she exclaimed breathlessly, "when you could be downstairs playing cards with the rest of us?"

Henry glared at her, hoping she'd take the hint, but Trina was undeterred.

"You should be ashamed of yourself." She shook her head disgustedly. "I bet you're up here sniffing over those old letters of yours."

Henry continued to glare.

"Mind your own business, Trina," he choked out through tight lips. She rolled her eyes heavenward.

"All right. Fine, be a grump." And with that, she turned on her heel and flounced out. The door slammed behind her. Henry let out a long, exasperated sigh and then took out his letters again. He was not sniffing over them, he thought angrily. It wasn't his fault what had happened to him. It had been an accident. That was the truth. But after fifty years of being cooped up at the school, he thought he was allowed a little bad temper.

Fifty years was a long time to be left on his own—and who knew how much longer?

# Trina and Nelly

O nce upon a time, Trina was a very pretty girl with red hair and bright blue eyes.

She liked to wear her hair in braids. That was the easiest way to keep it out of her face. When she fell off the horse, her hair was plaited as usual. They carried her out of the ring and up to the infirmary. The doctor had left her as she was because there was really nothing to do for her. There had been no blood. "A very clean break," the doctor said. "A very clean break, indeed."

Trina's parents came to collect the body, and she was still in her riding habit and boots. Her mother thought she looked like a little angel. Her father cried.

And ever since that day, she had been here at New Newbridge. Waiting.

Trina hadn't changed much in death. She still liked to talk a lot and bother people when she felt it was her business to. That's why she got so annoyed at Henry when he was in one of his moods. He behaved like a big old baby. And when she tried to cheer him up, well, he just got nasty.

He didn't want to be cheered up. He liked wallowing. That was the problem, as far as Trina saw it.

The real kids were gone for the summer, and only the ghosts lived there now. Trina liked it better when the realies, as they were called, were around. It made her feel better about things. She could follow the girls around and get all the gossip just like when she had been alive.

But during the long summer months all she had for company were the others like her. It wasn't as bad as it sounded. For the most part, they were very nice. She even counted a few among them as her friends. Nelly, a girl about her age who had gone into anaphylactic shock after a bee stung her during a nature walk, was sweet.

They shared a room together in the disused West Wing dormitory.

The West Wing dormitory had been partially destroyed when a boy who shouldn't have been smoking had fallen asleep with a lit cigarette. Luckily, no one had been killed. But the West Wing was now uninhabitable. The school was always meaning to have it refurbished, but somehow there was never enough money. Sometimes an adventurous student or two would make a hideaway of the place, but so far no one had caught on that a whole gaggle of ghosts was living there.

Nelly was waiting for her at the bottom of the stairs. Her dark hair was cut short and made her look more boy than girl. She had on a pair of hiking boots and a yellow T-shirt that said HAVE A NICE DAY on it. She was reading a book—probably something about bugs. They were her favorite. She had planned to be an entomologist before the bee had killed her.

"So?" Nelly had her head cocked, waiting for an answer.

Trina shook her head. "It was a no-go," she answered.

Trina sat down on the second-to-bottom stair and

dejectedly put her chin in her hands. Nelly patted her shoulder.

"It's all right. Henry will snap out of it in a few days." Trina appreciated Nelly's pragmatism, and usually shared it herself, but she just had this peculiar feeling that Henry was getting worse, not better.

"But every time he gets in a funk, it's always just a little bit worse and lasts a little bit longer." Trina sighed.

She put her chin in her hands and sighed again. This time even louder. Realizing that Nelly wasn't going to answer her, she changed the subject.

"By the way, have you seen Thomas? We were supposed to play chess today, but I can't find him anywhere."

"Who?" Nelly said quizzically.

Unlike Nelly, Trina knew practically everyone at New Newbridge. She made it her business to know everyone else's business, so that way there were never any surprises.

"You've met Thomas a million times. He's the one who likes to hang out in the kitchen and watch Mrs. Marble bake pies," Trina added helpfully.

Nelly began to shrug, and then suddenly her eyes lit up. She had remembered something important about Thomas.

"I saw him come inside the West Wing earlier," she said, then squinted her eyes and bit her lip. "But he never came back out."

"That's strange," Trina replied. Unlike Henry, Thomas was extremely well mannered, never yelled, and was *always* exactly where he said he was going to be. Trina wondered if something bad had happened to him, then quickly put the thought away. Once you were dead, well, there really wasn't that much bad stuff left to happen to you anymore.

"Oh, that reminds me, I met a new girl today," Nelly said casually, her nose partway in her bug book again.

Trina almost hiccupped with excitement, the big news immediately making her forget about Thomas and the missed chess game.

"A new girl! We haven't had a new girl in *forever*," Trina said. "How do you think she died?"

Nelly shrugged her shoulders and went back to her book. Trina opened her mouth to say something else, but realized that Nelly was no longer paying attention.

Suddenly something white and fluffy blew across the lawn, catching Trina's sharp eye.

"What in the world . . . ?" Trina said as she put aside

her excitement about the new girl and floated toward the object. Nelly, her nose still in her book, didn't even notice Trina leave.

But before Trina could get close enough to see what the white fluff was made of, she was interrupted by the unexpected appearance of a tall, lanky man with dark hair, one of the teachers at the school, she remembered. She watched as he ran out from behind the West Wing, passed through Trina like she wasn't there (she wasn't, as far as he was concerned), and stopped short when he reached the place where the white fluff waited. When he was sure no one was watching (Trina didn't count because she was a ghost), he scooped up the fluff, stuffed it into his pocket, and ran back the way he had come.

"Hmm . . . that's strange," Trina said to herself as she watched the teacher's retreating back. When he had finally disappeared behind the burned-out building, she floated back toward the stairs. Sitting down on the step beside Nelly, Trina let her mind return to the important issue at hand: *the new girl*.

A new girl was something special, Trina thought happily, not including Nelly in her thoughts this time. She was going to have to meet the new addition as soon

54

as possible and find out *everything* about her. Nelly might not care that there was a new ghost in town, but *she* certainly did.

"Oh well, it looks like I've got my work cut out for me," she said with excitement to no one in particular.

At least, she thought she did.

# Things That Go Bump

Something not so nice was listening to Trina. It refuses to be named as of yet, but believe me, it's a pretty nasty piece of business. Better not to tangle with it, if you get my drift.

Anyway, as Trina spoke, it listened. Not really digesting what she was saying, just filing it away for later use. It did this because everything can be used at a later date. If you hold on to a bit of information long enough, it will ripen and bear fruit, even if at the moment you receive it, it seems only to be a spare little kernel of unimportant knowledge.

# Chipping Away
# the Beef

Well, the chipped beef was just as Noh had imagined it. And the something or other she had smelled was steamed broccoli and homemade dinner rolls.

Noh was in heaven as she scooped a huge ball of butter from the butter dish and glopped it on her already partially eaten dinner roll. As she ate, she subtly stole glances at her aunt. She made sure to take her looks discreetly between bites of soft broccoli and fluffy dinner roll. She didn't think her aunt had noticed her careful glances until, as dessert was being served (strawberry short-cake, if you must know), Sarah turned and gave her a wink.

At that moment Noh decided that her aunt was very much like a cat: They both were sleek and smooth and graceful, and as far as Noh knew, they both were gunning for nine lives. Oh, and they both had yellowy green eyes that didn't seem to blink as much as they should.

The dining hall was huge. So it was strange to have only five other people sitting at the table with Noh and her aunt instead of the hundreds of screaming kids the place was used to holding.

To Noh's left were the caretakers, Mr. and Mrs. Finlay. Mrs. Finlay was as straight as a stick—no, a stick bug. That's what her father would have said. He was forever giving people buggie nicknames—even people he didn't know.

It sometimes embarrassed Noh when they would walk down the street and her father would remark—rather too loudly—"Noh, turn around, doesn't that woman look like a giant pill bug?" She didn't mind her father teasing, but she just wished he did it a little more quietly so that no one would give them dirty looks.

Mr. Finlay was shorter than his wife, with a fat red mustache to match his fat red face. *Give him a few more years,* Noh thought, *and he can play Santa Claus at the mall.*

Next to Mr. Finlay was Caleb DeMarck, the physics

teacher for the upper grades. Noh thought he seemed strangely nervous—especially for an adult—and he barely said a word as they ate.

He was a tall, lanky man with a shock of black hair and blue-gray eyes that seemed to be locked on Noh's aunt. Not that her aunt noticed. In fact, she seemed to be purposely "not" noticing. Noh was gonna have to find out what that was all about. She'd never known her aunt to ever be rude to anyone intentionally. *Very strange. Very strange, indeed,* Noh thought.

On the other side of the table, next to her aunt, was the groundskeeper, Jeffrey Hull. Noh knew immediately that she liked Mr. Hull when he had told her to call him "Hullie" and definitely *not* "Mr." anybody. He had a wrinkled countenance and smiling blue eyes. He just seemed happy to be there, period. Plus, he had thirds of the chipped beef, beating Noh's seconds.

The last person at dinner was the cook herself, Mrs. Marble. Even though her husband was long dead, Mrs. Marble talked about him like he was still around. This made Noh feel odd at first, but after a while Noh began to just take for granted that he *wasn't* alive. Maybe this was something Noh herself should try. If she were

to talk about her mother as if she were alive, maybe she would forget that her mother was dead too. Well, it was worth a shot.

"That chipped beef was mighty good eatin'," Hullie said, patting his stomach happily. He was the last one to finish dessert because he had had two helpings. Mrs. Marble was tickled pink that he had enjoyed dinner so much. She kept chattering about what a good appetite he had—of course, not as good as her own husband's, but close.

Noh decided that now was as good a time as any to ask about the girl she had seen earlier in the afternoon.

"Excuse me, but I was wondering where the other kids are tonight?" She said this seriously, but Mr. Finlay laughed. Mrs. Finlay elbowed him.

"Why, the other children don't come to school until the fall," Mr. Finlay said, clearing his throat. Noh knew this and didn't like anyone taking her for a fool.

"I *know* that, but what about the girl I met at that old, burned-out dorm today? Who is she?" No one responded. Silence filled the void.

"What's wrong?" Noh asked haughtily. "Why're you all staring at me like I'm a mealworm?"

Her aunt came to her rescue. "There are no other children here right now, Noh. I don't know whom you saw. Maybe one of the children from the town?"

Noh glared at her aunt. "I don't think so," she countered. She was sure the girl was staying here at New Newbridge. She could feel it in her bones.

"Well, maybe what you saw, my girl, was a ghost," Hullie added seriously. There was something mischievous going on behind his eyes. Noh wasn't sure if he was teasing her or not.

Mrs. Finlay coughed. "Well, Mr. Finlay and I must be turning in for the night." The screech of their chairs made a dent in the silent emptiness of the dining hall. Then, without a backward glance, they were gone.

Noh stared at her remaining dinner companions. Mrs. Marble had gone to the kitchen with the dishes, so this left only her aunt, the physics teacher, and Hullie.

"Do you believe in ghosts, Noh?" Hullie asked, wiping a bit of strawberry shortcake from his bright red beard with his napkin.

"I believe in them," Caleb DeMarck jumped in, before Noh could even open her mouth to respond. "Energy

can never be destroyed, only re-formed." Caleb blushed as he realized that all eyes had trained themselves on him. He swallowed hard and looked down at his hands. The fingers were long and tapered like a musician's.

"The energy," he continued, still staring at his hands, "that makes up our person could become trapped in the earthly plane, unable to return to its source—"

"Kinda like damming up a stream," Noh interrupted excitedly. Caleb smiled at her, nodding his head. She realized that Caleb DeMarck might not talk much, but what he did say was pretty neat.

"I think if someone were so inclined, they might come up with an experiment to test this ghost hypothesis—," Caleb began, but stopped when he caught sight of Noh's aunt's disapproving stare.

"Experiments aside, I think that if there are such things as ghosts, Noh, then they are probably more frightened of you than you should be of them." Her aunt said these words as she pushed her chair back and stood up.

"I'm not scared—," Noh started, but her aunt gave her a look. Noh instantly closed her mouth.

"I think it's time to go back to your room, Noh," her aunt said in a soft, lulling voice. "You've had a very

long day, and I'm sure all the traveling has made you very tired."

Aunt Sarah was strangely right. Noh found that she could barely keep her eyes open. She yawned loudly, quickly clapping a hand over her gaping mouth.

"Okay, Aunt Sarah," Noh said sleepily. "Good night, Hullie. Mr. DeMarck."

The two men nodded their good-nights.

"See you in the morning? Bright and chipper?" Hullie smiled.

Noh could only nod sleepily as she followed her aunt across the room, out the door, and into the arms of the waiting night.

# Scary Things in the Morning

**N**asty situations look brighter in the light of the morn-ing sun.

      Now, this assumption is not always a truth. And it is actually quite false in this particular case.

Remember that nasty thing that liked to file away information for later use? Well, it had spent the better part of the morning sitting on a toadstool out by the lake. When it wanted to, the nasty thing could make itself quite small—good for sliding through rabbit holes and into people's ears.

It was pretending to be a toad so that it could eat flies with a long, winding tongue. Not that it couldn't eat flies any time it wanted to, but catching flies just wasn't as much fun without a great big lolling tongue to flick, flop, and twist about.

The nasty thing had no true shape. It had to make do with stealing other creatures' shapes when it wanted to be seen. Mostly it liked being left to its own devices, so it chose to remain shapeless. In this state it was like a clear, undetectable gas.

After filling itself with a number of fly souls, it ceased being toadlike. It returned to the school, settling itself into a crack in one of the exterior walls of the West Wing to take a nap and digest the fly souls.

The nasty thing subsisted on the souls of the creatures it captured—little creatures like flies and beetles and spiders. But once, a long time before it had found its home at the New Newbridge Academy, it had eaten something big. And it had never forgotten the taste—and the *power*. The magnificent power the "something big" had given it.

Now the nasty thing, asleep in its crack, woke up with a start. It smelled something. *Something big.*

It puffed itself up and slipped back out into the mid-morning air in search of its newly smelled prey.

  68

# No Noh

Noh woke up and stretched under her blanket. The sunlight streamed in through the window, hitting her right in the face. She didn't mind, though. It was warm and inviting and made her want to smile. She threw off the covers and slipped out of bed. The floor was cold on one foot, the rug warm underneath the other. She quickly brought the other foot onto the rug and wiggled her toes happily.

She looked around her new room and felt happy, happier than she had felt in a long time. Then suddenly she remembered the conversation she'd had at dinner the night before with Hullie and the physics teacher, Mr. DeMarck, and instantly her good mood dissipated.

Two thoughts crossed her mind at the same time:

(1) Had she *really* seen a ghost yesterday? And (2) If so, did that mean there was something wrong with her? From her experience, normal people didn't see ghosts—or at least, the normal people she knew didn't see ghosts.

She was cheered by the scientific part of her brain that said ghosts didn't exist and there had to be a logical explanation for the appearance of the strange girl she'd met at the burned-out dorm. Maybe she was a local girl who was just using the empty building as her secret hide-out. Or maybe Noh had just imagined meeting the girl. She did have a pretty active imagination, and it had been known to get her into trouble in the past.

Growing up, Noh had spent a lot of time on her own, and her imagination had been her only real friend. It wasn't her father's fault, really. He was a good dad. He always made sure that she had food to eat and a nice place to live with nice things inside of it to keep her occupied. And he loved her very much—*that* she was sure of. It was just that he was always so busy.

His work was very important and it took him away for long stretches of time. As a small child, Noh had had a succession of governesses, but once she was old enough to look after herself, she had asked her father to please let her stay alone. Since Aunt Clara wasn't there to tell him reproachfully that it wasn't a good idea for a child to stay on her own, her father had agreed.

Noh had become a very self-sufficient kid. She could do the laundry, cook breakfast, lunch, and dinner (eggs were her specialty), and make sure that the house was neat and tidy.

But even though she had liked being in charge of herself, now that she didn't have to worry about that stuff anymore, she felt like a giant weight had been lifted from her shoulders. She felt free.

And that's when the happiness quotient kicked in again. So, guilty that she didn't miss her father more (she knew he'd come and visit before the start of the school year) and happy that there was a logical explanation for the "ghost" girl, Noh got her clothes together—making sure that the evil eye stone was safely in her pants pocket for good luck—and trooped off to the bathroom to begin her day.

Her hair slicked back and wet from the shower, Noh stood in front of the mirror brushing her teeth. She counted to 120 before she stopped twirling the brush around her teeth and spit.

She put her toothbrush back into the small cubbyhole (with her name stenciled on it) in the corner of the bathroom. She had deposited her toiletries there the day before at her aunt's urging. She had grumbled about it then, but she had been so tired when they had gotten back from dinner that she wouldn't have brushed her teeth at all if her toothbrush hadn't already been there waiting for her.

Noh stared at herself in the mirror.

She knew that she wasn't the prettiest girl in the world—her biggish nose and pointy chin made her look rather old-fashioned—but there was really nothing to be ashamed of in her features. They were strong and suited her long face well. Everyone said that she resembled her father, but Noh couldn't help thinking that was because no one had ever met her mother. The only people in the whole world who had known Mabel (Harris) Maypother were her father and his two sisters. Well, Noh was pretty sure that there had been others, but those were the only ones Noh knew about.

Her mother had no other family. Her parents had

  74

died when she was twelve, and she had gone to live with her only other relation, a great-aunt who had been already half-deaf from age. The great-aunt had passed away two years before Mabel had met Noh's father, and that was that. Mabel had been, for all intents and purposes, an orphan.

Thinking absently about her mother, Noh picked up a comb and ran it through her stick-straight hair. There was so much static electricity in the air that her hair stuck to the plastic comb in unruly clumps. She pulled out her barrette, knowing from experience that static electricity hair liked to stick to your face if 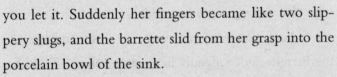 you let it. Suddenly her fingers became like two slippery slugs, and the barrette slid from her grasp into the porcelain bowl of the sink.

As if in slow motion, the silver barrette clattered against the smooth whiteness of the bowl and began to circle around the drain like a race car driver. Noh reached out her hand, groping for the barrette, but she wasn't quick enough. She watched in abject horror as the silver glinted once, then slipped down the drain.

"No!" Noh squeaked and stuck her fingers into the yawning mouth of the drain. It was cold and slimy to the touch, but Noh didn't care. She could just feel the barrette with the very tip of her fingers. She shoved her hand farther down the drain until she heard a small *click* and her fingers scissored around the barrette, dragging it back up into the light.

She grabbed the silvery hair clip with her other hand and moved it far away from the sink.

"I almost lost you," she whispered to the barrette, cradling it. It was a little dirty, but none the worse for wear. She wiped it off with her shirttail and slipped it into her hair. She was so happy to have her mother's barrette back in her possession that she almost didn't notice what the clicking noise had done.

"There, you're all safe now . . . ," she said again to the barrette, but suddenly her words trailed off. With a sharp intake of breath, Noh stared at the mirror. There was absolutely no reflection in it.

"Huh?" Noh gulped as she reached out a hand to touch the smooth sheet of unblemished silvered glass. It rippled as her fingers drew near it. She quickly pulled them away and looked around. She seemed to be alone in the bathroom, but she ran the length of the stalls just to make sure no one was hiding inside one of them. Satisfied, she returned to the mirror.

Instead of sacrificing her hand to the mysterious mirror, she took out her toothbrush and tentatively pushed it into the rippling glass.

It was halfway through the mirror when there was a sharp *crack* and Noh's reflection magically reappeared. She quickly tried to pull the toothbrush back, but the mirror had solidified around it. She grabbed the butt end of the toothbrush with both hands and yanked.

But her efforts were for nothing. The toothbrush was frozen solid.

She gave up her fight with the unyielding mirror and draped a hand towel over the protruding toothbrush. If she was lucky, anyone who came across it would think that she had suction-cupped a tiny hook onto the mirror's face. She didn't think it was a very plausible story, but it was all she had and she was sticking to it.

She quickly finished getting ready, then quietly slunk out of the bathroom hoping no one had seen her going in in the first place.

# The Crybaby

Henry was shut up in his room again. Not even Trina's needling would coax him out of his foul mood. As far as Trina and Nelly could see, this black funk had lasted twenty-two days, and the end was nowhere in sight.

Nelly sat on the floor watching a line of worker ants parade across the stone. They each had a tiny parcel of dried, flufflike substance in their pinchers.

"I wonder where they found this stuff," Nelly said as she chewed on the ends of her hair, watching them. She looked up at Trina, expectantly waiting for an answer.

"Looks like asbestos. I saw some earlier in the grass."

Nelly rolled her eyes.

"That's not funny, Trina—," Nelly started, but she

was interrupted by a loud wailing from up above them. Henry had started the final phase of his bad mood: the crying.

Trina sighed. "How many days does this part last again?"

Nelly thought for a moment. "It was three last time, but that's not saying much. The whole thing *only* lasted seventeen days last time. He's five days longer already."

Trina nodded.

Together, they waited for the crying to subside, but it was a futile attempt. Henry had had a strong set of lungs in his human life, and he still loved to use them. It was going to be a long next few days.

Nelly shook her head as the wailing increased and promptly disappeared into the ether. Trina stayed a while longer, hoping that Henry would tire himself out, but finally even she had had enough. The whole thing had given her a terrible headache.

She sighed and slowly faded into nothingness in search of a little peace and quiet.

At that very moment, the front door to the West Wing opened and Noh stepped into the semidarkness. She had armed herself with a flashlight and a sweater. She wasn't going to let the chill in the air keep her from investigating. She was determined to find out who or what the mysterious girl was once and for all.

Noh peered around the space and saw nothing out of place. It looked just like it had the day before. She walked to the staircase and ran a finger over the banister. It came away with a thick head of dust.

"Yuck," Noh squeaked, and wiped the dirt down the front of her sweater. Undeterred, she gingerly put her foot on the bottom step. It creaked with her weight but held firm. When Noh decided that the place wasn't going to fall down around her head, she began the climb to the second floor.

The stairs groaned with every step. She took the last few steps at a jog, happy to be on *almost* solid ground again.

Upstairs was just as unused and dusty as the rest of the place. She started down the hallway but stopped mid-stride when she heard a noise. She froze her muscles and stopped breathing so that she could listen more closely.

There it was again. And it wasn't just the building settling or an animal scampering across the roof. What

Noh heard was the sound of someone crying. It was the tail end of a long crying jag, so there was only a bit of sniffling and a few hiccups, but Noh would have known the sound anywhere.

She had spent many a long night crying herself to sleep. Usually it was when her father was away, but sometimes she found herself crying even when he was just down the hall. She wasn't a hundred percent sure why she did it, but she figured every so often you got so filled up with sadness that tears were the only way to feel any better.

She debated with herself for a few minutes, trying to decide if she should leave the crier in peace or just barge in and demand to know what the heck was going on. Finally, curiosity got the best of her. She walked down the hall and threw open the last door on the left, not knowing *what* she was going to find behind it.

# New Friends

**A**re you dead too?"

The boy who was occupying the dusty old room she had stepped into was about her age. She guessed that some people might think him handsome, but she found her first impression of him to be that of a big, sulky baby. She took in the red-rimmed eye sockets and tear-stained cheeks long before she noticed the large, well-lashed brown of his eyes, the square jaw, and the thatch of straight brown hair.

"No, I'm not dead," Noh replied. She didn't like having her leg pulled, and this boy was definitely trying to make her look stupid. "If you're dead, then you're not here anymore, and I'm right here," she said tartly, pinching her upper arm hard enough to make her grimace.

"See?" Noh waited for him to answer, but he just stared at her.

Finally, he shook his head and shrugged. "No, I don't see. I'm dead and I can pinch myself too, if I want to."

And he did.

Noh glared at him. "You are *not* dead. I'm not that gullible."

The boy cocked his head curiously. "What's 'gullible'?" At first Noh thought he was being a smart aleck, but then it dawned on her that he was actually being very serious.

"Gullible means that you believe everything that everyone tells you all the time," she said.

The boy scratched his head. "I don't think you're gullible, then. You don't believe *me*, even though I'm telling the truth," he said earnestly. "I wouldn't lie about something this important. Maybe you're dead and you don't know it yet."

Noh shook her head, but the boy didn't look convinced.

"Look, I would *know* if I were dead," Noh began. "I can promise you that—"

The boy interrupted her. "I've seen it happen before. Lots of times. No one really wants to be dead. They're scared of it."

He extended a hand toward Noh.

"I'm Henry."

"Noh. Short for Noleen."

She reached out a hand to shake Henry's but found, to her utter amazement, that her hand slid right through his.

"Oh, goodness!" Noh exclaimed. "You really are dead."

# Hasta La Vista Dead

Noh had never met a dead person before (except for the maybe-ghost girl she'd seen yesterday). She found that it was really no different from meeting a live person—except for the no-physical-contact part.

She and Henry spent the next few hours testing the dead/live waters. Henry made Noh walk through him (which she could do effortlessly), throw an inanimate object at his head (the pen from her pocket went straight through his nose and out the back of his skull), and try to guess a number from one to ten (this would have required a bit of telepathy—which, sadly, Noh did not possess).

"I never knew a living person who could see me before!" Henry exclaimed happily. The tears on his cheeks had long dried, and now his eyes glowed with excitement.

Noh shrugged. "Well, I think I might've seen at least one dead person before."

"Wow, I just wonder how it's possible. Maybe it's a miracle." Henry rubbed his hands together enthusiastically as he said this.

"I don't think it warrants being called a miracle, Henry. Maybe 'amazing' is a more apt word," Noh said thoughtfully. At least she knew that ghosts existed now, and even if that meant there was something different about her, well, she didn't mind it one little bit. It was better to be different and see ghosts than to be normal and not see them at all.

But, like Henry, Noh did wonder what it was exactly that had given her this strange new ability. She was curious to discover if other people could see both the living and the dead too, or if this was a gift that belonged to her alone.

Noh's stomach rumbled and she checked her watch. "It's almost twelve. I better go if I don't want to miss lunch. I think we're having apple pie for dessert."

As Noh started for the door Henry sighed jealously.

  88

"Boy, I wish I were human again. I haven't eaten a piece of pie in forever."

"At least you don't have to worry about your teeth rotting out of your head. I had three cavities the last time I went to the dentist," Noh whispered conspiratorially.

Henry grinned sheepishly at her. "I don't care. I still miss sweets . . ."

As Henry spoke, a strange breeze blew through the room, stirring up eddies of dust that made Noh sneeze twice in quick succession.

"What the—," Noh squeaked, looking around to see where the wind had originated from. She noticed immediately that all the windows and doors were shut up tight as drums.

"All of a sudden it's so cold in here," Noh said as she continued to sweep the room with her eyes.

Henry shook his head in agreement. "This is incredible. I haven't felt *anything* in such a very long time."

As if in response to Henry's words, all the drapes in the room rolled down, covering the windows and blocking out the ambient light. There was another sharp drop in the temperature, and Noh's teeth started to chatter.

"What's going on, Henry?" Noh moved closer to her dead friend, but his company did nothing to relieve the very bad feeling in the pit of her stomach.

"I don't know," he said through chattering teeth.

"Ghosts' teeth aren't supposed to chatter!" Noh said in a shocked voice. "At least, I don't think they are. I mean, I would guess that they shouldn't."

Noh shut her mouth, embarrassed by her nervous babbling. She kept silent as she watched Henry clench his teeth and squeeze his eyes tight. His shape seemed to flicker for a moment, but then he returned to normal.

"Should I try the door?" Noh said, walking toward it.

Henry shook his head. "I wouldn't bother. I just tried to disappear, but I couldn't. And that's never happened to me before."

"You tried to leave me?" shouted Noh. "That's not very nice!"

She stomped over to the door and put her hand on the knob. "We'll just see how you like it!"

She felt a prickly numbing in her hand and released the knob quickly. It was almost as if she'd run her hand under a hot *and* a cold tap at the same time. She held her hand to her chest, cradling it as it throbbed miserably

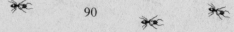

90

in time to the beat of her pulse. Without thinking, she reached into her pocket. The moment her fingers closed around the evil eye stone, the pain in her hand subsided.

At that very moment the wind picked up in earnest. Dust and pieces of litter, caught up in the wind's orbit, circled around their heads like tiny satellites.

"We've got to get out of here!" Noh shouted over the din.

"I think we're good and trapped!" Henry countered just as loudly.

Suddenly a small orb of light flared into existence in front of them and started to expand until it was as large as a doorway.

Henry sucked in his breath and drifted toward Noh. In a hushed voice he whispered, "It's my time. I have to go now." He dropped his hand on her shoulder in goodbye, but it only slid through her flesh.

"Wait, Henry! What're you talking about?" Noh tried to grab him, but he slipped out of her grasp and floated toward the glowing light.

"I only wish we'd gotten to be *real* friends," he said, his voice faint in the rush of the wind. When he reached the orb, he gave her a quick wave, then disappeared into the honeyed light.

"Henry!" Noh shouted, but she was too late. The light flared, and then the orb folded in upon itself and was gone.

Noh stared at the place where the light had once been, yet all traces of its existence had fled.

The temperature returned to normal, but Noh's teeth somehow wouldn't stop chattering. She looked down at her clenched fist, and it took her a moment before she realized she was clutching her evil eye stone as if it were a talisman.

Looking around the now empty room, it was as if the past few hours hadn't happened at all.

Noh sighed, upset that she had lost the first friend she had made at the New Newbridge Academy. She was just about to leave when she noticed a sheaf of yellowed paper sitting on the desktop. She picked it up and started to put it into one of the desk drawers when she became filled with curiosity.

Making sure she was unobserved, Noh stuffed the papers into her back pocket. She picked up her flashlight and walked to the door. She made a hesitant grab for the

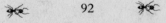

knob, and when it didn't hurt her hand, she threw the door open and stepped out into the hall. Not wanting to spend any more time in the West Wing than she had to, she made a run for the stairway. The thumping of her feet echoed in the empty building, obscuring the sound of Henry's bedroom door being slammed shut by a pair of unseen hands.

# Hullie Says

Noh hit the outside path at a run. She didn't look back at the West Wing as she ran, fearful that she would see something else "amazing" if she did.

She pumped her legs as fast as they would go. She didn't care if she got a stitch in her side or if her lungs collapsed from exertion.

When she got to the football field, Noh slowed to a jog and noticed for the first time how warm the day had become. She decided that going directly back to the dining hall would be a bad idea. She didn't want anyone to see her so spooked. She figured if she were to walk the length of the football field seven times (as seven was a lucky number), she'd be calm enough to return to normalcy.

"I can speak to ghosts, *and* the evil eye stone made my hand stop hurting," Noh said as she walked, even though there was no one around to hear her. "That has to mean something."

Sometimes when Noh was trying to find the answer to an important question, she would talk to herself out loud. Giving voice to her thoughts enabled her to sort out the helpful ones from the not-so-helpful ones. As she mulled over the two seemingly incongruous ideas, she got a tingly feeling all over. Instinctively she pulled the evil eye stone from her pocket and looked at it in the sunlight. It seemed to wink at her, as if to say that the answer she sought was right there in her hand.

Noh grinned as the solution hit her like lightning: *The evil eye stone has to be the catalyst for my new abilities!*

Noh wasn't one hundred percent certain that her hypothesis was correct, but she decided it would be smart to keep her new good luck charm close by just to be safe. She slipped the stone back into her pocket for safekeeping and continued her march around the football field.

Noh had almost finished her seventh lap when she heard a voice calling from the far side of the bleachers. She squinted into the sun and saw Hullie waving his arms wildly at her to get her attention.

He was too far away for her to hear exactly what he was saying, but Noh thought she could make out the words "lunch" and "hungry."

She picked up her pace and reached the grounds-keeper before he could say "Jack Sprat."

"You weren't waiting for me to get your lunch, were you?" Noh called out as she ran.

Hullie shook his head and smiled.

"Nope, I was just hoping we could have a few minutes to chat before we went in, that's all. I looked around for you earlier, but you had disappeared."

Noh fell into step with Hullie as they walked toward the dining room.

"Does this belong to you?" Hullie said as he pulled Noh's toothbrush out of his pocket and brandished it about like a sword.

Noh couldn't decide if she should fess up to being the owner of the toothbrush or deny it completely. She decided that honesty was her only choice because she sincerely liked Hullie and didn't want him to think she was a liar. Trust was a lot like lemonade. Once you

stirred in the sugar, it could never be unsweetened again.

"Um, yeah? . . . It's, uh, mine, I guess."

Hullie nodded and handed the toothbrush to her. She quickly pocketed it.

"Where did you get it?" Noh wanted to know. Hullie shrugged.

"Don't worry, my dear, it's our little secret." He gave her a pat on the shoulder, then pulled open the door so Noh could go inside.

"But, Hullie, the toothbrush was—"

Hullie put his finger to his lips to silence her as they rounded the corner and the massive double doors that led to the dining room came into view.

"We'll talk again later," he said. "The walls have ears, you know."

*At least I wasn't imagining things,* she thought as her nose followed the delicious food smells into the dining room. *There really are some strange and amazing things happening around here.*

Noh and Hullie were the last ones to come in for lunch. Everyone else had already eaten and returned to whatever work they were doing. Noh didn't mind. It meant that she could have seconds and thirds without feeling like a glutton.

She and Hullie tucked into their food in silence, both savoring the taste of the homemade meat loaf and garlic bread. When Mrs. Marble came out with hot apple pie for dessert, Noh and Hullie each had two pieces.

After Hullie had eaten the last bite of his pie, he wiped his mouth gingerly with his napkin and gave a polite burp, which made Noh giggle.

"Why don't we head outside and I'll show you where you can find a five-leaf clover," Hullie announced, setting his napkin on top of his empty plate.

Noh nodded, still remembering his comment about the walls having ears.

# Five-Leaf
## (or Six- or Seven-Leaf)
# Clovers

Noh followed Hullie out the double doors and across the lawn, her smaller feet taking *two* steps for every *one* of Hullie's.

"Where are we going, Hullie?" Noh said curiously.

He looked back at Noh and tapped his ear, reminding her to be quiet. She grinned and he gave her a wink.

After they left the lawn, they crossed the football field (the long way), went up and down the bleachers twice, walked back across the football field (the long way again), and then veered off into the woods. Noh followed Hullie in silence, her mind buzzing with all the questions that she wasn't allowed to ask just yet.

After a few minutes of walking through woods, with twigs and low-hanging branches grabbing at her face and arms, Noh and Hullie emerged by the lake. Noh didn't think she could *ever* retrace the path Hullie had taken—not even with a map that marked all the important places with big red Xs.

When Hullie got to the edge of the lake, he stopped and squatted by the water. He motioned for Noh to join him. She squatted down beside him, her brain itching to ask questions, but before she could open her mouth, Hullie beat her to the punch.

"This very spot is the safest place in the whole school to have a private conversation," Hullie said, smiling. "Remember that . . . *if* you want to keep your secrets while you're here."

"What makes it so special?" Noh asked. She couldn't even *begin* to imagine what made the spot such a great

place to have a private conversation. And Noh had a *very* good imagination.

Hullie didn't answer. Instead he looked down at the ground, his hand gesturing toward a small patch of green stuff that they just happened to be squatting next to. Noh hadn't even noticed it was there until Hullie pointed it out.

"These little *Trifoliums* are what make this spot so special," Hullie said.

"*Trifolium* is the Latin name for clovers," Noh replied, to Hullie's surprise. "My dad taught me lots of Latin names for plants and stuff. He's *really* a bug specialist, but he loves plants, too."

Noh looked at the green stuff closely, expecting to see a few mutants mixed in with a bunch of normal-looking three-leafers, but instead she found that every plant she saw was an honest-to-goodness five-leaf clover. And some of them even had six or seven leaves—which made them even luckier!

"Wow," Noh said. "This must be the luckiest place in the whole school!"

Hullie laughed.

"I think you just answered your own question, Noh," Hullie said.

It was true. Now Noh knew *exactly* why this was such a good place to tell secrets: It was lucky, and you always wanted luck on your side when you had important things to discuss but wanted to keep them private at the same time.

"Why are there so many of them?" Noh asked.

Hullie shrugged. "Nobody knows why for certain, but there is a legend about this place . . . ," he said.

Noh couldn't contain her excitement. She loved legends and myths. In fact, one of her favorite things to do was to curl up under the covers with a flashlight and *The Arabian Nights,* or a book about King Arthur and Camelot, and read all night long. She actually thought that when she grew up, she might want to write made-up stories exactly like the myths and legends she loved so much now.

"Do *you* know the legend?" Noh said, hoping very much that he did.

Hullie gave her a broad smile, letting her know that he *did* know the legend . . . and that he was going to tell her all about it.

# The Legend

"It happened during the New Newbridge Academy's first dedication ceremony," Hullie began, taking out a thin, carved toothpick and sticking it in between his teeth.

"The boy's name was Hubert," Hullie continued, "and he was overlarge for his age. This made people assume that he was older than he really was, and since they thought he was older, they treated him like he was older too. Which for some kids would've been the greatest blessing in the world, but for a boy like Hubert, well, it was really a *curse*."

Noh could see Hubert in her mind's eye. Instead of a normal-looking boy, she imagined a giant with fists like meat tenderizers and a head like a gigantic watermelon.

She could see exactly why he got yelled at more, why he got teased more, and why he was expected to behave better more. She completely understood why, as far as Hubert was concerned, everything was *more, more, more, more, more*—and not in a good way.

"As he got older, Hubert became more and more reserved," Hullie said, chewing on the end of his toothpick in exactly the same way that Noh chewed on the ends of her pencils. "He very rarely spoke unless spoken to, and he never yelled. *Never. His* thinking was that if he could just make himself smaller and quieter than everyone else, people would forget he was there and they would leave him alone."

Noh's image of Hubert changed. She now saw a little boy who just wanted to be left alone, hiding behind a giant *shadow* of himself. Noh understood wanting to be left alone. She knew how much easier it was to get by in the world when you pretended like you

didn't exist. Being a shadow lingering on the sidelines was usually how Noh liked to appear when she was around kids her own age. That way no one teased her or poked fun at her name—not that she let that bother her too much—but it also meant that no one asked you to join the kickball team or do a science project with them either.

"How did he do it?" Noh asked curiously.

"Well, when someone told Hubert that the Native Americans had perfected a way to walk without a sound so as not to scare away the animals they were hunting," Hullie said, "he read everything he could about them. And the more Hubert read, the more he wanted to be as silent and invisible as an Indian brave stalking his prey."

Noh wished *she* were an Indian brave. She and Hubert were in direct agreement about how cool *that* would be.

"Pretty soon Hubert had all but vanished," Hullie continued, still chewing on his toothpick. "He could go into any room in his house and no one would even look up. He could walk into any store and take what he wanted, and no one was ever the wiser. In fact, he was so invisible that he stopped showing up to school and

the principal never even called his parents. His curse, he decided, was now a *gift*."

"But was he really invisible?" Noh asked. She'd heard of lots of strange things—and seen lots of strange things too (like her friend Henry!), but she'd never ever heard of anyone learning to become invisible.

Hullie didn't speak immediately. Instead he tilted his head to the side and squinted his eyes, thinking. Finally, he shook his head like he was shifting his thoughts all around inside it and said, "Well, I can't rightly say."

"*I* think he wasn't *really* invisible." Noh shrugged. "I think he just wanted to be so badly that he *made* everyone around him *believe* he was. Kind of like an optical illusion!"

"Maybe so," Hullie said. "Maybe so . . ."

"Invisible or not, what happened to him next?" Noh asked, picking a six-leaf clover and twirling it between her fingers.

Hullie continued, "When Hubert heard about the dedication ceremony for the new school, he decided that this would be the ultimate test of his invisibility. He would attend the ceremony, and at the pivotal moment—when the mayor was *just* about to cut the

ribbon officially dedicating the school—Hubert would slip up to the podium, walk right past the mayor, and cut the ribbon himself."

"That's audacious!" Noh said, liking Hubert's plan *very much*.

"Well, if all went as planned, the audience would be so shocked to see a ribbon cutting *itself* that they would think the school was haunted and no one would ever let their children go there," Hullie said, adding, "he would be single-handedly responsible for closing the New Newbridge Academy before it had even opened."

Noh's twelve-year-old mind thought it was the most brilliant and dastardly plan that had ever been conceived. She wished she'd thought of it herself—not that she disliked people enough that she wanted to scare them all so badly.

"Did it work?" Noh asked.

"I'll let you be the judge," Hullie said, biting his toothpick thoughtfully before returning to the story.

"Hubert spent almost two months working on becoming even more silent and invisible than he already was. There was only one problem, one *thing* that Hubert was unaware of, and this one thing would be Hubert's undoing—but we'll get to that part later," Hullie said ominously.

"So, the day for the dedication ceremony came, and Hubert got up bright and early, brushed his teeth, and prepared for his big day. He spent almost two hours in the woods behind the school, practicing his Indian brave walk before he finally made his way over to where the dedication ceremony was being held in front of the new building."

Noh could just see Hubert creeping up to the place where the ceremony was being held. He would be the first person to arrive, of course, except maybe for some old handyman setting up chairs on the lawn for the day's festivities, but Noh figured that the old handyman would never even know that Hubert had ever been there at all.

Noh pictured a small stage where, hung between two wooden stakes, was the pièce de résistance of Hubert's plan: a bright yellow ribbon, rippling in the wind. The setting couldn't have been more perfect for what Hubert had planned, Noh decided. She bet he could hardly wait to put his insidious plot into motion.

Hullie cleared his throat, bringing Noh back to reality.

The stage disappeared from her mind, and Noh looked down to see that she had dropped the little six-leaf clover on the ground at her feet.

"Go on," Noh said. "What happened to Hubert? Did he do it?"

Hullie chewed on his toothpick, clearly enjoying the suspense he was creating. "Hold your horses, girl, give me a moment. It's a long story and I want to make sure I get all the details right."

Noh sighed. She hated waiting. If there was one thing she definitely needed more of, it was patience.

"Now, then," Hullie said, finally continuing the story. "The dedication ceremony went on for a zillion years—or at least, that's what Hubert thought. The mayor droned on about how nice it was to have the New Newbridge Academy in the community, and the man who had given all the money to build the school got up and thanked the mayor and the community for being so nice themselves.

"All the self-congratulating just made Hubert glad he'd come up with his plan in the first place. Finally, when Hubert was absolutely sure the mayor was going to go on *another* twenty zillion years, the mayor's assistant

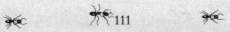

suddenly got up and handed the mayor the biggest pair of gardening shears Hubert had ever seen.

"Instantly Hubert was on the move. If he timed it just right—and luck was on his side—he would get to the stage right before the mayor snipped the ribbon. Hubert moved silently through the crowd, invisible to all the people he passed."

"Did he do it?!" Noh asked. She had been so caught up in the story that she had almost forgotten to breathe.

Hullie shook his head sadly.

"It made Hubert feel very special to be able to do all this right under everyone's noses, and this feeling of 'specialness' was Hubert's downfall. You see, just as Hubert was stepping up onto the lip of the stage, right before he could reach out and yank the ribbon out of the mayor's grasp . . . something *strange* happened.

"The ribbon that had just been quietly rippling in the breeze only moments before suddenly shot up into the air, twitching like a wild snake about to strike. The mayor, who didn't know that Hubert was there, thrust his garden shears right at the rippling ribbon snake, lopping it cleanly in half. The crowd got to its feet and gave the mayor a standing ovation."

"Oh no!" Noh said, fear spreading through her body. Quickly she thrust her hand into her pocket and grasped the evil eye stone. Immediately she felt calmer.

Noh swallowed hard and nodded. "I'm okay, Hullie. Go on."

Hullie sighed. "I'll tell you what happened next, but I don't think you're going to like it very much."

Noh didn't think she was going to like it very much either, but she knew from experience that most stories didn't have a happy ending—no matter how much you wished they did.

"Hubert sat down on the stage between the mayor and the crowd, but nobody saw him," Hullie said quietly. "Nor did anyone see him when he crawled off the stage and across the lawn, cradling his arm to his chest

  113

as he tried not to look at where the garden shears had lopped off *all four of the fingers on his right hand.*"

Hullie paused before continuing.

"Hubert made it as far as the lake before he collapsed. Then he just sat there, not sure what to do to make the blood stop leaving his body. He knew he needed help, but he had been invisible for so long that he didn't think he could make anyone see him . . . *even if he wanted to.*

"The hours passed slowly, and Hubert got colder and colder until he stopped being able to feel anything at all. Because of this sad fact, he didn't even notice when the last drop of blood left his body."

# Detective Noh

"That's a terrible story," Noh said.

No one deserved to die like that, she thought, alone and invisible. Hullie seemed to agree with her.

"It is, but, alas, that's the legend," Hullie said, shaking his head. "They say that because *luck* felt so bad about what had happened to Hubert, it made the very spot where he died the luckiest place in the school."

Noh looked down at all the five-leaf (and six- and seven-leaf) clovers and felt that Hubert's death was a very high price to pay for them.

"It's still a terrible story," she said.

Noh sat in silence, continuing to digest what she had just heard. Even though it was a sad story, it did give credence to all the strange things she had already encountered at the New Newbridge Academy.

She knew there were ghosts inhabiting the school—a bunch of them, actually, but all that was just the tip of the iceberg. There was a whole lot more going on at this school than anybody realized. Well, maybe a couple of people knew what was what—like Hullie, for one—but everyone else mistakenly thought New Newbridge was just a regular old scholarly institution.

"Hullie, have you seen the ghosts?" Noh asked suddenly.

The older man shook his head and Noh sighed thoughtfully.

"Now, wait a minute. I may not have *seen* anything, but I've been the groundskeeper here for more than twenty-five years, and, let me tell you, I've *heard* some pretty funny stuff," Hullie said as he picked out a nice big seven-leaf clover and held it between his large fingers.

This was just more confirmation that Noh was on the right track, that the evil eye stone had special powers. Because, unlike Hullie, she'd *seen* some pretty funny stuff in the past twenty-four hours—like ghosts disappearing forever and toothbrushes stuck in mirrors.

"It's mostly out in the West Wing, but there's lots of strange things happening all over the school," Hullie added, interrupting Noh's thoughts of free-floating toothbrushes.

"This school is special, isn't it, Hullie," Noh said softly. She wasn't asking a question—she was making a statement because she already *knew* the school was special. The evil eye stone had shown her this truth. She just didn't know *why*.

"'Special' is the word." Hullie laughed. "I guess it's just one of those big mysteries you have to go and solve for yourself."

"A *mystery* . . . ," Noh whispered under her breath. That's exactly what it was: a mystery that had Noh's name written all over it. It would be her summer project. She would solve the mystery of the New Newbridge Academy, and her good luck charm would help!

"Thanks, Hullie!" Noh said as she got up and started walking back toward the school, taking the widest steps her legs would make.

"Thanks for what?" Hullie said quizzically.

But Noh was too busy thinking about solving mysteries to reply.

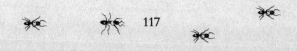

# The Something Big

The nasty thing that does not wish to be named would like you to know that once upon a time—because it has no real recollection of time or space—it ate something big. It doesn't want you to know *what* that something big is right now, but it *would* like to stress the fact that the something big was, well . . . big.

*Really, really, really, really, REALLY BIG.*

# Into the Light

Henry was gone.

Trina had looked *everywhere*, and he was absolutely *nowhere* to be found. She knew she was probably overreacting, that Henry had to be *somewhere* on the school grounds, but since Henry never went *anywhere* under normal circumstances, it did seem a bit strange that he hadn't been in his room in the West Wing when she went looking for him earlier.

And on top of all that, she hadn't seen Thomas, either. She didn't want to think about what *two* missing ghosts might mean.

She had a bad feeling in the pit of her stomach—the kind of feeling that, when you were alive, made you want to go lie down so you wouldn't throw up your lunch. Her tummy felt all bubbly and syrupy inside, like she was a soda can someone had shaken so hard, it was about to burst.

Trina loved adjectives. She could make the juiciest sentences with them, sentences all about how uncomfortable her tummy felt—or really about *anything* she was feeling. She had even won a number of Juicy Sentence Awards in school before she had died. Her parents had been so proud of her that they'd hung the awards in the living room so that everyone who came to visit could get an eyeful of them.

Nelly—who was of the "less is more" school of thought—always made a sour face when Trina launched into her juicy sentences. She said that Trina used too many words. To prove her point, Nelly always tried to use one sentence to describe something that would take Trina three whole pages of notebook paper to explain.

This never bothered Trina, but to make Nelly happy, she took to saying her juicy sentences to herself, using as many similes and metaphors as she could in her head so that no one ever knew she was the queen of juicy sentences at all.

Juicy sentences aside, she really *did* have a bad feeling

in the pit of her stomach. And it wouldn't go away, no matter how much she reassured herself that Henry was perfectly fine, wherever he was. She just didn't believe her own words.

Unable to keep her worries to herself, Trina went looking for Nelly. She found her friend outside, crouched down in front of a large bayberry bush.

"What're you doing?" Trina said as she plopped down beside Nelly and looked over her shoulder.

"Watching ants," Nelly replied, her eyes trained on the snaking line of worker ants, each insect weighted down with a piece of white bread–looking stuff.

"Asbestos again?" Trina asked curiously, forgetting all about Henry's absence for the moment.

"No, something from the cafeteria, probably," Nelly answered. She hadn't looked up at Trina once, but she did scratch her arm three times, Trina noted.

"I guess it does look like bread. They seem to really like

the stuff," Trina said, but all Nelly did was shrug. They sat there, staring at the ever-lengthening line of ants for a long time until Trina remembered why she had gone looking for Nelly in the first place.

"Henry's gone!" she shrieked suddenly. "And so is Thomas."

This made Nelly look up from her ants and blink twice, like she'd just seen something that had blinded her.

"They're gone and I think something terrible has happened to them—something *really* bad. I can feel it in the pit of my stomach, like it's a soda can about to burst," Trina finished, glad that she'd told someone else because now her tummy felt slightly better.

"Did you look all over the building?" Nelly asked.

Trina nodded. "I looked everywhere!"

And she really had. When she couldn't find Henry in his room, she'd looked in every corner, every dark spot, every secret place in the West Wing. She'd been dead awhile, so she knew all those places like the back of her hand. She couldn't find a trace of either boy—although she had seen the dark-haired teacher again skulking around outside the West Wing. He didn't have any of the asbestos-bread-fluff with him, but there was still

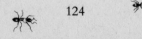

something kind of suspicious about him lurking around the burned-out old building.

"What about the rest of the school grounds?" Nelly asked after Trina had stopped talking.

"Well, um . . . ," Trina stammered. It was the first time in decades that Trina remembered being at a loss for words.

"Yes . . . ?" Nelly said, encouraging Trina to continue.

"I don't really like to leave the West Wing," Trina said sheepishly.

"You're outside now," Nelly said, looking around at their surroundings.

Trina blushed an even deeper shade of red.

"Yeah, but you're with me."

She hated to admit this to her friend—because it made her look like the biggest baby in the whole world—but the truth was that Trina was deathly afraid of being alone outside of the West Wing.

When she'd first died, she'd been entirely carefree, unafraid of anything, but as time had gone on, she'd started to develop the feeling that if she spent too much time away from the West Wing, she'd become one of those ghosts that . . . *disappeared*.

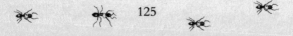

She really hoped something nice happened to you after you disappeared. The ghosts that had gone into the light hadn't seemed scared, but she knew in her heart that she wasn't ready for whatever lay ahead. All she wanted to do was stay at New Newbridge as long as she possibly could.

And if sticking close to home helped make that happen, well, she was just gonna stick as close to home as possible.

Nelly made a sour face and turned back to the ants. She didn't have much use for fears and phobias and definitely didn't think that encouraging Trina's would be a good idea.

"I'm sure they're both around here somewhere," she said finally, her eyes scanning the line of ants for any sign of the queen. She had a feeling that the queen of this busy ant kingdom had to be pretty smart because her worker ants moved with such precision and dedication that it was almost like they were in the military.

"Maybe," Trina said, sensing that she would get no further help on the subject from her friend.

*Or maybe not,* she thought.

She rather hoped she wasn't right.

# Catherine Alexander

**W**henever Noh had a problem that she didn't know the answer to, she would ask her dad for help. When *he* didn't know the answer, he would direct Noh to the only place in the whole world that *did* have all the answers to everything: the library.

Noh loved the library in her town. It was bigger than the fire station but smaller than the grocery store. It was made of warm brown brick, and it always seemed to be inviting you inside when you looked at it.

She had spent many a rainy day ensconced in one of the large, overstuffed armchairs that littered the science section, reading up on weird diseases and perusing whatever fiction tome had happened to catch her fancy when she wandered through the literature section. She had made

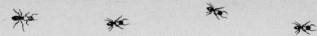

her way through all the Anne of Green Gables books and every Jane Austen novel she could find while sitting in those overstuffed armchairs. Just thinking about their lop-sided gray cushions put a smile on her face.

So that's how Noh found herself standing in front of the giant, carved wooden doors that led into the inner sanctum of New Newbridge's library. If she knew anything at all, it was that somewhere inside the library waited her best chance at cracking the mystery.

Noh pushed open the door with a loud *creeeak* that almost gave her a heart attack. She felt like she was in one of those scary black-and-white monster movies her dad liked to watch late at night when he thought she was asleep—except this was *real* life, not TV.

The space was much bigger than she'd imagined—three ominous-looking rooms in total—and chock-full of dusty old books that looked like no one had touched them in a thousand years. She closed the door behind her with another loud *creeeak*, but this time she was prepared for the sound, so it didn't make her heart do somersaults again.

The library seemed empty, with a fine layer of dust on *everything*.

"Hello . . . ?" Noh called out, even though under normal circumstances she wouldn't have made any sounds louder than a whisper in a library.

No one answered her. Not even the squeak of a mouse or the crunch of a shoe sounded in the emptiness. Noh took this as a sign that it was okay to enter. Her thoughts were that if someone wanted the place to be off-limits, then they'd have locked the doors.

Noh tiptoed across the front entryway, her shoes making little *squeak-squeak* noises as they moved across the dark blue marbled floor. Noh thought that there had to be some kind of pattern built into the marble, but the slabs of dark blue and green were so squiggly and strange that she just couldn't make out their code. She wondered if she were to climb the large circular staircase that stood against the back wall up to the second floor, if she would be able to see whatever picture the marble spelled out.

Taking the rickety wrought-iron stairs two at a time, Noh made it to the second-floor landing in less than ten seconds. She walked over to the balustrade and looked down.

What Noh saw made her head hurt and her eyes swim. It was a great big mishmash of color that would

have been at home in the middle of an abstract painting, but seemed *very* wrong for the floor of a school library. Noh put her hand to her head and leaned against the railing. She felt like she was going to be sick right then and there.

*"What are you doing?!"* called a shrill voice from the first floor.

Noh squinted down at the circulation desk, and sitting squarely behind the counter was the largest woman she had ever laid eyes on. The woman was wearing a bright blue and green muumuu that matched the colors of the floor, making her seem to almost blend in with the pattern. Noh supposed that that was why she hadn't noticed the woman in the first place. Although it did seem strange to Noh that the woman hadn't said a word when she'd first called out her "hello."

131

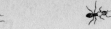

Noh's head cleared and she was able to stand up straight again. All the dizziness seemed to have disappeared at the woman's words.

"I was just looking for a book," Noh said, even though that wasn't the complete and utter truth. "And then I wanted to see what the floor looked like from up here, so I climbed up the stairs."

"And how *did* the floor look from up there?" the woman said, cocking an eyebrow with curiosity.

Noh swallowed hard.

"Like an abstract painting."

The woman nodded, then said, "Are you sure about that?"

Noh almost rolled her eyes with frustration. She may have been a kid, but she wasn't blind.

"Why don't you take another look?" the woman said before Noh could say another word.

Noh didn't want to look at the floor. In fact, she would've rather eaten a tub of live cockroaches than look at the floor again, but she also didn't want to seem like she was a scaredy-cat, either.

"Okay," Noh replied, and gulped hard. She took a deep breath and looked down at the floor.

"That's not right!" Noh said loudly. "It wasn't like that before."

What Noh saw now when she looked at the floor was wall-to-wall ugly beige marble. There was no dark blue or dark green anywhere and definitely no pattern that made your brain spin inside your head.

"It's always been this way," the woman said as she picked up a book and stamped it with a big black stamp. "Why don't you come down here and tell me your name."

"But the floor was different—," Noh started to protest, but the woman put a finger to her lips.

"Shush now, girl, you're in a library."

Feeling silly, Noh took the stairs one at a time, dragging out how long it took to reach the bottom. When her toes touched the floor, she realized that it felt very different than it had before. Her shoes no longer made a *squeak-squeak* sound as she crossed the marbled floor, and the layer of dust that had been all over the library seemed to have vanished.

The whole thing was very *suspicious*, as far as Noh was concerned.

The woman was waiting for Noh when she reached

the circulation desk. Even though Noh wanted to dislike the woman for making her feel so stupid, she found herself instantly liking the wide, triple-chinned face; the long, black hair that was so black, it almost looked blue; and the bright violet eyes that seemed to brim with curiosity.

"I'm Catherine Alexander, the head librarian at New Newbridge," the woman said, sticking out her humongous hand. "You must be Noleen-Anne. Your aunt has told me so much about you."

Noh stuck out her own hand and took Catherine's. The skin of the large woman's fingers was soft and warm as she engulfed Noh's hand in her own. She gave Noh a good, strong shake, then let her go. Noh could feel the reverberations of that handshake all the way up her arm and down her spine.

"Now, tell me, Noleen-Anne," the big librarian said in a feathery whisper, "how would you like me to help you decipher that sheaf of papers you have crammed into your back pocket?"

# The Lemon Solution

Catherine Alexander took the frayed papers that Noh handed her and spread them out on top of the polished oak circulation desk, where they mixed in with all the rest of the papers on top of the desk.

"Looks like a letter . . . to a fellow called Henry . . . from his mother," Catherine Alexander said thoughtfully. "But this last one's blank." She suddenly lifted the page to her nose and gave it a giant sniff.

"Hmmm," Catherine Alexander said, wiggling her nose and giving the paper a curious glance. This *hmmm* was very thoughtful as well.

Next she took a loupe—Noh knew that this was really just a tiny magnifying glass, because her dad used one for his work—that was attached to a long silver chain from her shirtfront pocket, and she leaned forward to examine the papers, placing the loupe right up to her left eyeball.

Noh, who didn't have her own nifty magnifying glass, squeezed one eye shut (the right one) and put her head down next to Catherine Alexander's. When she got bored with looking at the words that had been painstakingly written across the yellowing sheets of paper in long, looping cursive, she tilted her head so she could watch the librarian.

The magnifying glass made Catherine Alexander's eye seem ten times bigger than it actually was. Noh wanted to laugh at how silly the librarian looked, but since the large woman appeared to be very seriously involved in deciphering the papers, she was afraid to even let out a giggle.

Catherine Alexander cleared her throat twice, then made a low *hmmm*ing sound down in the bottom of her throat. She took the loupe from her eye and offered it to Noh.

"I want your opinion on this," Catherine Alexander said, pulling out the last page, the one that was blank, and helping Noh put the magnifying glass to her own eye. Noh had a feeling her eyeball looked just as big and funny as Catherine Alexander's had only a few moments earlier.

Noh closed her right eye so she wouldn't see double and peered down through the magnifying glass. She blinked twice, expecting to see something strange about the paper, but all she saw was nothing—just a lot bigger.

"I don't see anything," Noh said with disappointment as she lowered the loupe from her eye.

"Exactly!" Catherine Alexander said happily. "*Nothing.* That's exactly what I thought too."

She picked the lone paper up off the desktop, carried it across the room, and stopped at one of the polished oak reading tables. She pulled the lampshade off the table light and laid the paper on top of the bare bulb. Noh trailed a few steps behind her, totally baffled by what the librarian was doing.

"Just as I suspected," Catherine Alexander said, squinting down at the paper. "Come look."

She motioned for Noh to look at the paper as it baked over the lightbulb.

"Wow, that's amazing!" Noh said, shaking her head to make sure she wasn't imagining things, because her mind was definitely having a hard time believing what her eyes were seeing. Scrawled across the page, completely covering the whole page, was another letter! Only upon closer inspection, Noh realized that it wasn't a letter at all, but a bunch of weird scientific notations. Decimals and fractions littered the page, but there were lots and lots of numbers, too.

"Invisible ink. Lemon juice, I think," the librarian said.

"But why?" Noh asked. "What's so important about a bunch of numbers that someone wanted to hide them like that?"

Catherine Alexander made a tut-tutting sound.

"I believe that this blank piece of paper houses an important secret. I don't know how it got mixed up with your friend Henry's letter, but somehow it did."

"What kind of secret?" Noh said uncertainly. She wished now that she liked numbers *half* as much as she liked words so she could understand the secret too.

"These aren't just numbers, Noh," the librarian said, shaking her head. "They're equations. And if I'm not mistaken, they may turn out to be even more important than I suspect."

# Inside Out

The West Wing was awash in ants, and Nelly had been the only one to notice it. All afternoon she'd monitored the ant army as it had amassed its troops in the foyer, and she had waited for them to do something that would explain *why* they had all decided to meet here in the burned-out West Wing.

Her eyes goggled in astonishment as she stared at all the insects marching by her feet. She realized that she had never seen so many of the little suckers in one place at one time in her whole life (or death). Of course, being the avid arthropod lover that she was, she'd had an ant farm back home in Michigan before she'd come to the New Newbridge Academy, but her extra-large plastic terrarium was *nothing* in comparison to this. There were so many ants that she couldn't have counted them all, even if she'd wanted to.

Nelly wasn't sure whom she was supposed to tell this important ant army information to—it wasn't like when she was in school and could just tell a teacher whenever she had a problem. Nope. Now that she was dead, she was on her own.

When she'd tried to point out the ants' strange behavior to Trina, her friend had only made fun of her, teasing her about the hardworking ants eating asbestos—*like they don't know asbestos is poisonous! They're ants, not dummies,* Nelly thought angrily.

But she knew better. She suspected that these ants were up to something . . . something *different*. And she was determined to discover what that something different was.

So while Trina had looked for Henry—he hadn't been in his room, where he normally hid out during his nasty black moods—Nelly had gone off to find the answer to the ant army mystery. Besides, the search for Henry hadn't really interested Nelly all that much, anyway. She'd always liked insects way better than people— and you could go ahead and lump ghosts right into the *people* category, as far as she was concerned.

In the end, Nelly hadn't had to do too much discovering. She'd just followed the line of ants all the way out to where it started by the lake. She'd stood by the edge of the water and watched as more and more ants trooped out of the woods and joined the ever-growing line.

Next she'd followed her own footsteps back to the West Wing, stopping to examine the place where the ant line curved by the archery field, because there seemed to be a smaller line of ants intersecting the bigger line there. She'd wanted to follow the smaller line back to where it started, but something inside her brain told her that it was a dead end, that the ants were going to the New Newbridge Academy, and it didn't matter one little bit where they were coming from.

When she got back to the West Wing, she did what she *should* have done in the first place: She looked to see exactly where the ants were going. She followed the line over to the base of the brick fireplace that stood across from the portrait of the school's first trustee, Eustant P. Druthers, and found that, one by one, the ants were disappearing into a small hole in the hearth just below the fireplace grating.

After that, Nelly could find no trace of the ant line, no matter where she looked.

She was so busy trying to discover exactly where the ants were going that she didn't notice the cold at first, but gradually she realized that she was feeling something she hadn't felt in a long, long time.

"What in the—," she started to say, her teeth beginning to chatter like a pair of windup teeth as all the drapes in the foyer dropped down, blocking out what little light was sneaking into the room through the windows.

It was so cold that when Nelly looked down at the ant army, even the insects seemed to be shivering on their stalklike legs. Suddenly a strange silence filled the empty air. Nelly looked up and saw a shimmering, golden orb materializing by the fireplace. As she stared at it, it grew larger and larger, until the orb was just big enough for Nelly to climb through.

She floated toward it, her mind and body drawn to the glowing thing like a kid to candy. Obviously, it was her turn to enter the light.

She wondered if when she got to the other side, her old dog, Brandy, would be there to greet her. She'd been so heartbroken when a car had hit the big golden

retriever just days before she'd gone off to start her first year at the New Newbridge Academy.

It was a strange last thing to think, she decided, because she hadn't thought about Brandy even *once* in almost fifteen years.

As she felt her essence beginning to merge with the glowing orb, Nelly had another strange thought. And for the death of her, she couldn't have said where it came from.

*What if this isn't the real light but a fake light? One that doesn't lead to the other side but to somewhere else entirely?*

And then she was gone.

144

# Up and Down
the Stairs

Catherine Alexander had declined to go with Noh to Caleb DeMarck's office. She said that she preferred staying in her library, where she always knew what was just around the corner, but she *had* given Noh a note to give to the physics teacher, explaining the urgency with which the librarian hoped he would decipher the equations that she and Noh had discovered.

Feeling like she was finally getting somewhere with her detecting, Noh walked out of the library, making sure to close the giant doors quietly behind her. Catherine Alexander had drawn a map for Noh, pointing out the way to the physics teacher's office, but the more she walked and tried to follow the librarian's directions, the more confusing the map became.

When she had first watched the librarian writing it, the map had looked very simple, a few directions here and there and a drawing or two. Yet every time Noh consulted the map for the next direction, the more directions there seemed to be. No matter what Noh did—whether she took a right turn at the atrium or a left turn at the basketball court, or took three sets of staircases up and two sets of staircases down—she found herself right back at the front entranceway to the main building.

The whole thing made Noh's head hurt.

Finally, after what seemed like hours, Noh opened the front door and went outside. She sat down on the steps that led to the main building and scratched her head. She wanted to crunch the map up into a tiny little ball and eat it. Maybe that way the map would get into her bloodstream and help her go the right way. She was almost tempted to go back to the library and ask the giant librarian why she'd given her a trick map, but she felt silly accusing someone of something that she wasn't sure of. Maybe the map *was* really just a map and the problem was all in Noh's head. She thought back to the cemetery she'd gone into after she'd left the train station. Hadn't she had the same problem there? She'd had to go

out the way she'd come in because she couldn't get to the other side—and she definitely hadn't had any kind of map then.

The idea that she might be "directionally impaired" made Noh's tummy feel funny, like she'd eaten too many desserts.

She got up and stretched like a cat, deciding to try to get to the physics teacher's office from another direction. Maybe if she went to the back entrance of the main building, she'd have better luck.

Trina had gone too far from the West Wing. She could feel it in her nonexistent bones. She'd been so busy looking for Henry and Thomas that she'd strayed all the way over to the main building.

"Henry!? Where are you!" she called one more time, her voice as chirpy as a baby bird's. The more nervous she got—and she was starting to feel *very* nervous— the higher and more stretched her ghostly vocal cords became. If she didn't find the boys and get back to the West Wing soon, her voice was probably going to fly away.

"Hey—*who* are you looking for?" a voice said from

behind her, frightening her so badly, she nearly disappeared. She tried to place the owner of the voice, but she couldn't—which was strange because she knew nearly *all* the ghosts at New Newbridge.

*Wait a minute,* Trina thought. *There's one voice I don't know: the new girl's!* She had been so preoccupied that she had totally forgotten what Nelly had said about there being a new ghost at New Newbridge.

"You're the new girl!" Trina said excitedly as she turned around and found a small, dark-haired girl about the same age as herself standing across from her. This new girl had a jacket wrapped around her waist, even though it was summer.

She'd probably been dead since the fall, Trina thought, and hadn't even known it—hence the jacket.

The two girls stared at each other, a kind, welcoming smile on Trina's face and a curious, pinched look on Noh's.

"How do you know I'm new here?" Noh asked uncertainly. There was something about the redheaded girl in the jodhpurs and riding helmet that seemed *off* to Noh—she just couldn't put her finger on what it was.

"Oh, Nelly told me all about you," Trina said brightly, forgetting how only moments before she had

been so worried about being far away from the West Wing. A new ghost at New Newbridge was an exciting thing. And as far as she was concerned, *this* new girl looked *very* promising, indeed.

"Is that the girl who kept scratching her arm?" Noh asked. She was almost certain that it was.

Trina nodded happily.

"I thought so," Noh said. She had been right. All the kids she'd met so far at New Newbridge were ghosts. That's how this girl knew Henry . . . because she was a ghost too!

"By the way, were you looking for a ghost named Henry?" Noh asked, hoping it was a different Henry from the one she'd met earlier—even though she knew it wasn't.

Trina nodded again, her riding helmet bobbing up and down on her brightly colored head. She was so pale-skinned that Noh could see tiny reddish-brown freckles dotting almost every square inch of exposed skin on the girl's arms and face.

"I hate to have to tell you this, but he's gone," Noh said finally.

"Gone?" the girl said, cocking her head curiously.

The look on her face reminded Noh of a dog: one who'd just been scolded and didn't know why.

"I just met him—he was crying in a room upstairs in the West Wing, and while we were talking, it got really cold and then a glowing orb appeared and he said it was his time," Noh babbled, not sure if the other girl was even listening.

"His time?" the girl repeated. She looked even more confused than before.

"That's what he said," Noh offered. "And then he went into the light and disappeared."

The other girl's eyes got as wide as saucers and she stopped blinking. She opened her mouth to speak, but nothing came out.

"I'm sorry," Noh said, feeling like that last bit of slime at the bottom of a slop bucket. "Are you okay?"

The girl nodded, then suddenly disappeared.

# Ghost to Girl

Sorry about that," the girl said as she magically reappeared in front of Noh. "I just wanted to check something out."

"Oh," Noh said. She didn't know if she should be annoyed with the girl or not. She *did* think it was kind of rude for someone to simply disappear like that without telling you first.

"I wanted to ask Nelly something, but I couldn't find her anywhere," Trina said. "By the way, my name's Trina. What's yours?"

"Noh."

Trina scrunched her eyebrows together.

"Well, that's a funny-sounding name," Trina said, then clapped her hand over her mouth with embarrassment.

It was only *after* the words were out of her mouth that she realized how rude they sounded.

Noh glared at her. Glaring was something Noh hardly ever did. She was a pretty easygoing girl, but when someone poked fun at her name, it made her so mad that she wanted to scream.

"If my name's funny-sounding, then so is yours," Noh declared, her eyes narrowing. She wanted to say something else, something mean that would put the weird ghost girl in her place, but she knew it was wrong. It was okay to defend yourself, but if you took it any further than that, then you were as bad as the other person.

Trina clasped her hands together and looked squarely into Noh's eyes.

"You're right. We both have strange names."

Noh had been prepared for a fight. Now she didn't know *what* she was supposed to do—she hadn't expected the other girl to agree with her like that.

"I'm sorry I was rude," Trina continued, "but you said something that spooked me and I wasn't really thinking right."

"It's okay," Noh said grudgingly. "I didn't mean to upset you, either."

Trina gave Noh a smile, but her lower lip was quivering.

"I just can't believe Henry's gone. He was kind of mean sometimes, but he was my friend."

Noh felt like she should tell Trina that she was sorry her friend was gone, but no words would come out of her mouth. She decided that words didn't say enough. Instead she pulled the paper that was with Henry's letter from her back pocket and handed it to the ghost girl.

"What's this?" Trina said as her lower lip instantly stopped quivering and her eyes lit up with curiosity.

"It's a secret code," Noh offered mysteriously. "I'm taking it to the physics teacher so he can tell me what it means."

Trina scrunched her eyebrows together. She didn't know how to explain to Noh that the living didn't see the dead. Surely the other girl had realized at least this much . . . but no, if she *thought* she was alive still, well, that put things in a different light entirely.

"I don't know if that's such a good idea," Trina said finally. She decided that honesty was the best policy in this situation.

"Why not?" Noh said. Did the ghost girl know

something about the physics teacher that she didn't know?

"Well, I guess the best way to say this is with the truth," Trina said. "You're dead, Noh, and as hard as that is to believe—"

Trina wasn't prepared for the loud *snort* that popped out of Noh's nose. The snort immediately turned into a giggle, then a belly-burning guffaw, and finally, big, wet tears began to roll out of the corners of Noh's eyes and down her cheeks. Trina didn't know what to do. She hadn't meant to make the new girl cry.

"I'm so sorry. I know it's really a terrible thing—"

This just made Noh laugh/cry harder.

"Please . . . ," Noh said between sobs and loud gulps for air. "Don't talk . . ."

"But I—"

"Please . . . no more . . . stomach hurts . . . it's gonna . . . burst . . ."

Trina nodded, working very hard to stop herself from saying anything that would make Noh's stomach burst. This was very hard for her because Trina loved to talk more than anything in the whole world. In fact, asking Trina not to talk was like asking a normal person not to breathe. It was kind of impossible.

"I just—," Trina said, not able to help herself. This made Noh—who'd just begun to calm down—start laughing/crying all over again.

"Sorry!" Trina yelped, feeling awful. She and the new girl had gotten off to a terrible start. She just hoped Noh didn't believe all that hooey about first impressions being the most accurate—otherwise, she would *never* want to be Trina's friend.

Finally, Noh stopped laughing enough to explain to Trina why she had started laughing in the first place.

"It's just that all the ghosts here at New Newbridge seem to think *I'm* a ghost too, just because I can see them," Noh told Trina, who only looked confused. As far as Trina knew, Noh being alive *had* to be an impossibility. Trina had been dead for a *pretty* long time, and *she'd* never met a living person who could see ghosts before.

"I don't know about that," Trina said. "Maybe you *think* you're alive, but you're *really* dead."

Noh shook her head.

"I'll prove it to you," she said.

As Noh reached out to shake Trina's hand, Trina gasped. Noh's fingers went right through her own. Trina took a step backward, and if she hadn't been floating an

inch above the ground, she'd have tripped over a rock and fallen on her butt.

"But . . . but . . . but that's impossible," Trina stammered. "You're not a ghost . . . ?"

Noh shook her head. At last, Trina seemed to be getting the point.

"Oh my goodness," Trina continued, comprehension dawning on her face. "You're a . . . *realie*!"

# No Apologies

The nasty thing that refuses to be named would like to interject something at this point in the story. It wants you to know that when you read the next few chapters, you will not think very well of it . . . *and that the nasty thing feels perfectly fine about this.*

It wants you, the reader, to know that it doesn't care one iota *what* you think of it. It says that "it is what it is" and that you are just going to have to deal with it.

# Caleb DeMarck

I 'm going with you," Trina said, and no matter what Noh did, the ghost girl wouldn't take no for an answer. That's how Noh ended up at the physics teacher's office, trying to listen to what he was saying about the secret code while she glared at a ghost that no one else could see, who wouldn't stop talking and distracting Noh from the business at hand.

When Noh had knocked on Caleb DeMarck's office door, the physics teacher had immediately opened it and ushered Noh inside. It was a large office with carved wooden panels running up and down the walls.

The place was a mess. There were papers everywhere—on the big wooden desk, on both of the chairs that stood in front of the desk, all over the floor, and covering the

tops of two large metal filing cabinets. Caleb DeMarck had gestured for Noh to take a seat, but she declined, worried that she'd disturb whatever creature might be living underneath all the mess on the chair.

Instead she'd remained standing, handing him the note from Catherine Alexander and waiting for his response. After reading it, he'd wanted to look at the secret paper right then and there. Noh fished it out of her back pocket and handed it to him.

He was so excited by his first glimpse of the mathematical equations that littered the page that he almost tore it in half as he yanked it out of Noh's hand.

"That was weird," Trina said as the physics teacher began to devour the equations like jam on toast—which reminded Noh that it was getting close to dinnertime and her tummy was starting to rumble.

The teacher's hands began to shake as he became more and more engrossed in what he was reading.

"Ask him why he was wandering around the West Wing," Trina said suddenly, but Noh had no idea what she was talking about and ignored her.

Noh knew that she shouldn't feel so annoyed at Trina—the ghost had directed her right to Caleb

DeMarck's office without making her go up or down any flights of stairs at all—but the silly girl wouldn't stop talking. At first Trina just made quiet asides to Noh, commenting on how nervous the physics teacher looked, or how messy his office was, but then she started bugging Noh to ask him questions about his whereabouts, and that's when Noh wanted to strangle her.

Finally, Caleb DeMarck looked up from the letter, and if Noh hadn't known better, she'd have thought he was hiding something. His pupils were larger than they'd been before, and he had a shifty look on his face.

"Well, I think our librarian may have jumped to conclusions . . . ," he began, his hands still clutching the letter like a security blanket.

"Ask him why they used lemon to hide the equations," Trina said, distracting Noh and making her miss the physics teacher's next words. "Just ask him. It might be important. Oh, and don't forget to ask him about the West Wing!"

Noh was trapped between a rock and a hard place. She couldn't tell Trina to be quiet because Caleb DeMarck didn't know the ghost was even there, and she couldn't ask the physics teacher to repeat what he was saying

162

because then it would look like she had the memory retention of a peanut.

"I'm sorry, Mr. DeMarck," Noh said, interrupting Trina *and* the teacher at the same time. "I don't understand. What *does* Ms. Alexander think the equations mean?"

The physics teacher laughed, and it was such a weird, strange laugh that it made the hairs on the back of Noh's neck stand at attention.

"Why, our librarian seems to think that these equations might be part of the lost files of our school's first trustee and cofounder, Eustant P. Druthers. He was an amateur inventor, an inveterate explorer . . . *and a genius*," Caleb DeMarck boomed, his eyes shining.

"He's weird," Trina said in a small voice. "Especially his laugh."

Noh glared at Trina before turning her attention back to the physics teacher.

"Wow, that's cool, but what do the equa—," Noh started to say, but was interrupted halfway through the word "equation."

"You have to understand that he was a great man!" the physics teacher continued. "You wouldn't know

much about him since he was such a private person, but he did amazing things. . . ."

The physics teacher talked for a long time, extolling the numerous feats and virtues of Eustant P. Druthers. Noh started to get the impression that no matter what she did, she was never gonna get the answer to her question.

"Let's get out of here," Trina said with a yawn. "We can go back to the West Wing and find Nelly and maybe go to—"

But Noh quickly shook her head. Caleb DeMarck had just said something that had piqued her interest.

". . . and he also equipped the school with all kinds of secret passageways and hidden rooms," the physics teacher said as he nervously scratched his nose. "But don't tell anyone I told you that. I could get into a lot of trouble."

Noh's stomach rumbled, but she ignored it.

"Secret passageways?" Noh asked. She had a feeling that she might have already come across one of them back in the girl's dormitory bathroom earlier that morning. Which meant that Hullie knew all about the secret passageways and hidden rooms, because he'd found her toothbrush stuck in one of the entranceways.

"There are lots of them sprinkled around the school,

but none of the students are supposed to know about them, so not a word," the physics teacher said quickly, his eyes darting around the room.

"Since you don't think that paper is part of the lost collection, could I have it back?" Noh said suddenly.

"No!" he said loudly, then cleared his throat and said in a much less angry voice, "I think I'd better hold on to this for a while."

"But if it's not important . . . ," Noh said with a sharp smile.

The lanky physics teacher didn't say another word— he just pulled open the top desk drawer, set the paper inside, and shut it with a firm *click*. He took a key from his pants pocket and locked the drawer.

"I'm confiscating this paper," he said, fixing Noh with a steely eye. "And if you make a big stink about it, I'll tell them that I caught you trying to steal it from me in the first place."

*That's cheating,* Noh thought angrily, but she knew better than to press her luck. Caleb DeMarck was not the sort of a person that he had appeared to be. There was nothing gentle or meek about the rude man sitting behind the wooden desk.

Trina echoed her thoughts.

"Adults shouldn't lie," Trina said hotly. "That's, like, against the law!"

Noh agreed with her. Adults should be setting a good example—especially teachers—for the children around them, but Noh was fast discovering that the world was a very different place from what she had originally thought.

"Do I make myself understood?" Caleb DeMarck said, his eyes fixed on Noh's. She nodded but didn't say a word.

"Good. Now, it's almost time for dinner, so I suggest you go to the cafeteria and forget all about finding that paper."

Once again, Noh only nodded.

From the way she was nodding, most people—this included the spiteful physics teacher Caleb DeMarck—would think that Noh had given up, that she had put the memory of finding the equation-covered paper into a secret drawer in the back of her brain and locked it away, never to be seen again.

But they would be wrong. Noh held her tongue for one reason and one reason only.

She was busy formulating a plan.

# A Dip in the Pool

Noh's plan consisted of three things:

1. Missing dinner
2. Being observant
3. Not telling a *living* soul one little
   thing about her plan.

"But how do we *know* he's not going to dinner?" Trina asked for the third time since Noh had explained the plan to her new friend.

Noh sighed. She hated overexplaining things, especially plans. She imagined that plans were like falling stars. They just happened near you, and if you questioned them, they disappeared. In the past she hadn't had to explain anything to anyone because she had spent most of her time by herself, and when she hadn't been by herself, she had been with her father . . . and he would *never* have asked her to explain anything private like that.

Besides, overexplaining just made everything all muddled inside your brain.

"We *know* he's not going to dinner because he specifically told *me* to go there so I wouldn't be in his way," Noh said for the third time. Trina nodded, but she still didn't look convinced.

"I think he's hiding something for sure," Trina said. "Nelly and I saw him skulking around the West Wing *twice*!"

Suddenly Noh heard a sharp *click* and she sat up expectantly. Her legs were cramped from sitting in the janitor's closet across from the physics teacher's room for so long, but she ignored them, excited to finally put her plan into action. She eased open the door and almost screamed when she saw Trina waiting on the other side.

*Sorry,* Trina mouthed as Noh glared at her. She wasn't used to ghosts disappearing and reappearing all over the place. Trina pointed down the hall just in time

   168

for Noh to see Caleb DeMarck rounding the corner and disappearing into the dark.

"He's getting away," Noh hissed, trying not to make *squeaky* sounds with her sneakers as she jogged down the hall in the same direction the physics teacher had just gone.

Trina disappeared again, but then Noh caught sight of her ghost friend down at the end of the hall, gesturing for Noh to follow her. Noh decided that in the future she wouldn't get so frustrated with Trina's quirks. Without her ghost friend's special abilities—being able to disappear and reappear wherever she liked—Noh would've probably lost the physics teacher's trail, wrecking the whole plan.

Noh followed Trina through three or four long, winding hallways, across a darkened classroom, down two flights of stairs, and into the gym. When she crossed the threshold into the gym, her sneakers squeaking on the polished floor, she saw the safety lights shining onto an empty basketball court. She looked around for her ghost friend, but Trina was nowhere to be found.

Noh was startled by a loud grating sound that filled the empty space, and the whole place began to vibrate.

Noh watched in awe as the gym floor started folding in on itself. She quickly stepped backward, her feet making loud squeaks on the slippery floor as she scampered for the doorway that led out of the gym. She had barely reached firm ground when the mechanized floor evaporated right out from underneath where she'd just been standing.

"Wow," Noh said under her breath as she stared at the Olympic-size swimming pool that had been revealed by the floor's disappearance. She started to take a tentative step toward the empty pool but stopped in her tracks when she spied Caleb DeMarck coming out of the locker room across from her, a gleeful smile plastered on his face.

He walked along the edge of the pool, paused where it was shallowest, and climbed down inside. Noh watched as he crossed the pool floor and crouched beside the exposed drain.

Once again, Noh wondered where Trina had gone.

She found that she was missing the ghost girl's company more than she realized.

When Noh turned her attention back to the physics teacher, she saw that he was on his hands and knees now, pulling hard on the top of the drain. When nothing happened after a few moments, he sat up and scratched his head. He tried a different tack. This time he pressed his fingers against the drain, probing here and there until Noh heard a tiny *crunch*. She watched in amazement as the drain began to sink into the concrete.

"It's one of those secret things," Trina whispered into Noh's ear, making her jump.

"Where were you?" Noh whispered back. Trina frowned.

"I was looking for Nelly, but I can't find her anywhere. And none of the other ghosts I've talked to know where she went," Trina said, her eyes wide with fear. "I think . . . I think she might've *gone*."

"Like Henry?" Noh said, careful to keep her voice low. Trina nodded.

"And my friend Thomas, too," Trina said.

There was another *crunch*, which attracted the girls' attention, and they both looked down to see that the

drain was completely gone and in its place was a massive hole . . . but where was the physics teacher?

"I'll check on him," Trina said, disappearing again. Noh waited for Trina to report back. When the ghost didn't return in a prompt manner, she stepped out of the doorway and walked over to the pool.

She had a funny feeling that whatever Caleb DeMarck was doing down there . . . *it wasn't something good.*

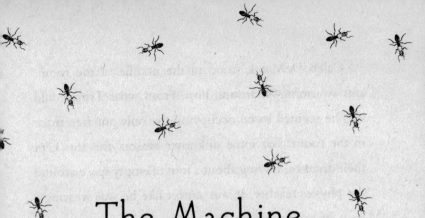

# The Machine

There were ants everywhere. If Trina hadn't been a ghost, and therefore safe from having to touch insects and other creepy, crawly things, she would've run screaming from the room. As it was, she wasn't really *happy* about having to make her way through the mass of wriggling, squirming ants, but at least she didn't have a body for them to climb all over.

The hidden room wasn't very large—probably the size of an old World War II bomb shelter, except that it was completely empty (if you didn't count the ants, the physics teacher, and a large metallic machine that stood in the very back). The walls were made of cut stone, and there was one bare lightbulb hanging from the ceiling, illuminating the whole space.

Caleb DeMarck stood in the middle of the room, ants swarming all around him. From what Trina could see, he seemed to be occupying the only ant-free space in the room. For some unknown reason, the ants kept their distance, leaving about a foot of empty space around the physics teacher. It was almost like he was wearing a layer of extra-strength "instant death" bug spray instead of cologne.

Trina moved farther into the room, invisible to Caleb DeMarck and the ants. Even *if* she had been a living, breathing girl, the ants and the teacher were so focused on the large circular machine that took over the entire back part of the hidden room that they wouldn't have noticed her anyway.

Trina had no idea what the machine had been used for, but she decided that it had to have been a dazzling silver color in its youth. Too bad it was so tarnished with age now that it looked dark bronze. It consisted of two large electrodes that sprouted from a squat round frame, and each electrode had three long wires running out of it that reattached down at the base of the machine. There was also a long silver lever soldered to the center of the machine, which Trina figured must be the on/off switch.

The ants seemed to think that the room and what was hidden inside it belonged to them. They swarmed all over the place, making the bottom half of the machine appear alive with movement.

As Trina marveled at the strange sight Caleb DeMarck pulled the secret paper that Noh had given him out of his shirt pocket and opened it. His eyes gazed at the mathematical equations with wonder, with every blink drinking in the lemon-juice ink code that Catherine Alexander had broken.

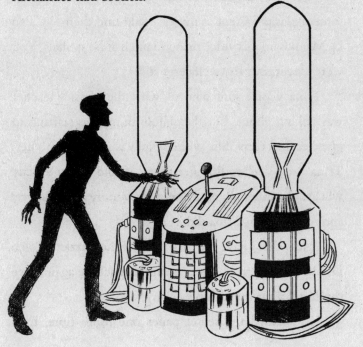

Trina assumed that the physics teacher had no idea that she was even in the room, so when he started talking, it startled her.

"You don't even know what I've done!" he said, his tone full of excitement.

It took Trina a moment to realize that the physics teacher was talking to himself and not to her, making her giggle with relief. Meeting one realie who could see her was more than enough to last Trina a death-time.

"You left the clues, hidden so ingeniously that only someone as persistent as myself could find them," Caleb DeMarck said, his voice rising in pitch as he spoke. "You were clever, but I was cleverer still."

Trina wasn't sure who or what the physics teacher was talking about, but the whole thing was starting to give her the creeps. She wished Nelly were here with her. Trina had a feeling that her friend would know exactly what to do. After all, Nelly knew way more about insects and science than Trina did.

"Now that I have the final piece of the puzzle," Caleb DeMarck continued, his eyes on the machine again, "we can fulfill your invention's *destiny*."

He scanned the secret paper one more time, then

pulled something white and fluffy from his pants pocket and sprinkled it in front of him. The ants greedily grabbed at the white stuff—the same stuff Trina and Nelly had seen the ants with earlier—and Caleb DeMarck took a step toward the machine. The ants cleared a path for him as quickly as their little legs could carry them. In that instant, Trina realized that the ants were under the physics teacher's thrall!

Whatever that white stuff was, *it was making the ants do anything Caleb DeMarck wanted them to do.*

Trina watched as the physics teacher reached for the wires running out of one of the electrodes. He consulted the secret paper, then pulled two wires out of their sockets and switched them. Satisfied, he stepped back and reached for the silver lever sticking out of the machine's belly. There was a loud *crunch* as he pulled the lever down. The machine roared to life, the two electrodes buzzing with electricity.

Without even realizing what she was doing, Trina took a step backward. There was something about the machine that terrified her, even if she couldn't have said precisely what it was. She just knew instinctively that she needed to get out of that room as fast as she possibly could. She closed her eyes, imagining herself back in the burned-out West Wing's foyer. Then she opened her eyes, expecting to see the portrait of the school's cofounder, Eustant P. Druthers, staring at her.

Instead Trina found herself right back in the hidden room. For the first time in a very long while, Trina's hands felt cold. She looked down at them, but they looked exactly the same: slightly translucent. A shiver ran down her spine—another feeling she hadn't experienced in a very long while—and her eyes widened in fear. There was a giant glowing orb slowly unfolding itself before her eyes. She found herself entranced by the light. It was so beautiful. She didn't know why she'd been afraid of going into it before. If she'd known how pleasant the whole thing was, she might well have welcomed it happening to her.

Trina slowly started to float toward the orb, her thoughts becoming muffled the closer she got to it. She was almost to the edge of the light when she heard someone calling her name. She didn't want to turn around and see who was calling her. She wanted to go *into* the light.

*"Trina!"* the voice called, louder this time.

She turned her head, her eyes searching for the owner of the voice.

*"Don't do it! It's a trap!"*

Trina's gaze landed on Noh.

*"Trina, come back!"* Noh screamed, her face pinched with worry. She stood directly behind Caleb DeMarck, who didn't seem to have the least clue to whom Noh was talking. He looked around the room blankly, an expression of befuddlement on his face.

"Turn off the machine!" her new friend cried, pushing past the startled physics teacher and reaching for the silver lever.

"Don't touch that!" Caleb DeMarck shouted, pulling more of the white stuff from his pocket and sprinkling it on the floor. Noh's fingers had just grasped the shiny switch when she started to shriek. Trina looked down and saw that both of Noh's legs were now covered in a swarm of squirming black and red ants.

Since Noh was so busy with the ants, her hold over Trina slackened and the call of the orb overwhelmed the ghost again. Trina turned away from her ant-covered friend, her eyes searching for the beckoning light. She saw that the orb was even larger than it had been before, even more luminescent . . . *and without hesitation she began her journey into its shining depths.*

# Explanation: Part 1

Noh had been bitten by ants before, but never so many at the same time. She was tempted to reach down and squish the little buggers with her palms, stopping the nasty ant pinchers from embedding themselves in her skin, but she knew she had bigger fish to fry, and time was of the essence. Ignoring her stinging legs, she again grasped the silver lever sticking out of the base of the machine and pulled it. In the blink of an eye the silvery orb disappeared and Trina turned around, her eyes wide with shock.

Noh let out a loud sigh of relief, but then the pain hit her. She angrily started slapping the biting ants with everything she had. Caleb DeMarck, who up until that very moment might as well have been a statue for all the

good he had done, scattered more of the fluffy white stuff at Noh's feet. Almost instantly the ants ceased attacking Noh, and the ones that hadn't gotten mushed crawled off her legs, swarming around the white stuff like it was manna from heaven.

Somehow just knowing that the ants weren't covering her legs anymore made Noh feel a lot better. Her skin still stung from the twenty or so ant bites she'd received, but she knew she'd heal.

"Thank you," Noh said, even though it had been the physics teacher's fault that the ants had attacked her in the first place. She reached down to scratch the most painful bite on her kneecap, knowing all the while that she shouldn't, then returned her gaze to Caleb DeMarck.

"I don't understand your thinking, Noh," the physics teacher said. "What right did you have to interrupt my experiment?"

Noh didn't know where to begin. She was torn between telling the physics teacher *exactly* what he'd almost done and . . . well, there really wasn't any other option than the truth.

"I don't know what that machine does," Noh said,

pointing at the tarnished metal thing in the corner, "but whatever it is . . . I think it sucks up ghost energy."

The physics teacher opened his mouth to speak, then immediately shut it again. He looked *very* confused.

"Ghost energy?" he said finally, his face turning white.

"Ever since I came to New Newbridge, I've been able to see ghosts. I've met three of them personally, and I think there may be a lot more," Noh said, preparing herself for the worst. There was no way in a million years that the physics teacher was gonna believe her story— even if it *was* the absolute truth. She wished she had a truth-telling machine so that she would never have to worry about adults believing her stories. She decided that if this situation was only going to end badly, she might as well tell the physics teacher *everything*.

*"Um,"* Noh continued, "you should also know that there's a ghost here in the room with us right now. Her name is Trina and I think your machine almost ate her."

The physics teacher's face got even whiter.

"You said that the machine almost ate the ghost?" Caleb DeMarck repeated, his eyes searching for some sign of a ghostly presence. "How?"

  183

It had taken a couple of minutes for the effects of the machine to wear off, but now Trina was mad. Since she was feeling more like herself again, she opened her mouth and started doing one of the things she did best: talking.

"Tell him about the orb and the light and the—," Trina began, but Noh held up her hand.

"I'll tell him everything, Trina," Noh said to her friend. "I promise, but just let me think for one minute."

The ghost girl nodded, remembering that she owed Noh her ghostly existence since she had stopped the machine from gobbling her up.

"If you tell me what you think the machine *does*, I might be able to explain how it works," Noh offered after she'd taken a moment to put things in perspective. She didn't have all the pieces to the mystery, but she knew that once Caleb DeMarck gave her a couple more clues, she'd be close.

"Well," the physics teacher began proudly, "many years ago, when I was a student here, I stumbled upon something special, something secret at New Newbridge. I think I have to start there for you—and your friend—to understand."

# The Know-It-All

Caleb DeMarck had a hard time making friends. He just couldn't understand why no one liked hanging out with him. He would have been very surprised to discover that it was because the other kids at New Newbridge considered him a know-it-all.

And not only was Caleb a know-it-all, but he was the worst *kind* of know-it-all. He was always the first kid to shake his head and snicker at anyone who admitted that they didn't know something. He made the other kids in his class feel dumb when they got an answer wrong, or when they didn't get an A++ on a test.

The saddest part of the whole thing was that Caleb didn't even know *he* was the cause of his own problems. He just assumed that it was the other kids' faults, that they were mean-spirited or jealous of someone who was smarter than them. He had no idea that that was exactly how the rest of the school saw *him*: mean-spirited and petty.

Since Caleb didn't have any friends, he spent most of his time in his room, reading books and doing science experiments. It was during one of these experiments that he discovered a way to make his own friends.

New Newbridge has always been home to many different kinds of insect life. Every creature that creeps, crawls, or slithers is represented in some capacity at the school. You just have to go off on an insect expedition into the woods and you'll find praying mantises, crickets, ladybugs, lizards, and spiders galore—and that's just the tip of the iceberg.

Yet, by and large, the real kings of New Newbridge have to be the ants.

There are at least nine colonies of black ants and seven colonies of red ants—and that's just on the school grounds. Go into the woods and there are many, many more. They do more business on school property—and give Hullie more trouble—than all the students and faculty combined.

In truth, they rule the school.

And that is precisely why, as a student at New Newbridge, Caleb DeMarck found the ants so fascinating.

He loved to sit outside and document their movements, tabulate how productive they were, discover where they made their nests. He found one aspect of their lives to be of particular interest, and this became the thing that he fixated on the most: aphid farming. Ants herded aphids in the exact same way that human beings herded cows and sheep.

Intrigued, Caleb collected specimens to study in his room. He made copious notes and drew numerous sketches. He did all the experiments he could think of to explain the strange relationship between ants and their aphid pets. Of course, it didn't take him long to realize that the ants had an ulterior motive for their aphid care and attention. Ants didn't simply herd aphids for fun, they herded aphids for milk! Just like humans milked cows, ants milked aphids.

More important, Caleb found that when this nutritious aphid milk was administered in high enough concentrations—something Caleb could easily create in the school lab—they became so addicted to the aphid milk concoction that he could basically make the ants do anything he wanted them to.

Thus began Caleb DeMarck's long-standing friendship with the ants, and it was through this relationship that Caleb discovered . . . *the machine.*

Caleb remembered the unusually warm day in March like it was yesterday.

Bored because it was a weekend and no one had asked him to join any of the Frisbee or touch football games outside on the school lawn, Caleb had followed the ants on an expedition into the school. For some reason, the ants ignored the cafeteria (which was their usual destination) and instead made their way through the building and downstairs into the gym. The swim team was preparing for the spring session, so the gym floor had been rolled away and the pool was empty, awaiting a good cleaning before it was refilled with water.

Caleb watched as, one by one, the ants marched down the side of the pool, across the pool floor, and into the shiny silver pool drain. Caleb had no idea where the ants were going, and he desperately wanted to find out, so he climbed into the empty pool after them.

He wasn't small like an ant, so he couldn't fit down the drain, but he had other skills . . . and one of those skills was using scientific reasoning to solve problems. He began pressing on the drain and then pulling on it where he could get a handhold. Suddenly without warning there was a loud *crunch* and the whole bottom of the pool began to descend.

Caleb stepped back away from the pit until he was sure that it was safe, and then he did what any other kid with a scientific mind would do: He followed the ants down into the hole.

# Explanation: Part 2

And that's how I found the machine. I don't know *exactly* what it does, but from what I've seen, it appears to create electricity out of thin air."

Caleb DeMarck looked down at his hands. He knew now that what he had said was *very* wrong. The machine *didn't* create electricity out of air . . . it created electricity out of *ghosts*.

"I spent years trying to figure it out, but it wasn't until recently that I discovered this," the physics teacher said, pulling Noh's secret paper out of his pocket.

"That's mine!" Noh said, her hands on her hips.

The physics teacher shook his head.

"No, *this* is your paper," he said, pulling *another*, matching sheet out of his back pocket. "I found the first one in some old papers I checked out of the library. I knew that it didn't contain the whole equation, but it was enough to get the machine up and running."

"Then why did you need that paper?" Noh and Trina said at the same time, overlapping each other. Of course, the physics teacher only heard Noh's question.

"I needed the secret paper you found to calibrate the machine properly," Caleb DeMarck said. "I adjusted a few wires here and there, and this time when I turned it on, I didn't almost freeze myself to death."

Noh didn't doubt his answer one bit. She remembered how terribly cold it had gotten when Henry had been sucked into the orb.

"We have to reverse the machine," Noh said. "You've been using ghost souls to power it and that's not fair!"

Noh expected the physics teacher to agree with her immediately, but instead a stubborn look spread across his features.

"How do I know that what you say is *really* true?" he said, his voice high and reedy like a petulant child's. "I can't see the ghosts, so you might be making the whole thing up. Maybe if you *showed* me the ghosts . . ."

Noh couldn't believe what she was hearing.

It seemed that deep down inside, Caleb DeMarck was still that know-it-all boy who was blind to everything but what *he* wanted.

And what he wanted right now was to see a ghost.

Noh knew the physics teacher wasn't a bad person on purpose, he was just too self-absorbed to see that he was the cause of all the trouble around him. Still, she didn't *really* want him to know about her evil eye stone. Sharing her secret with him might be inviting more trouble than it was worth.

But, she supposed, if she wanted to get Henry and the others back, she was going to have to take the plunge and do it.

"Okay," Noh said, starting to formulate a plan in her mind. "I can make you see the ghosts, but you have to do exactly what I say. No questions asked."

Excited by the prospect, Caleb DeMarck gave Noh an enthusiastic nod. The physics teacher seemed ready to do whatever she asked of him—Noh just hoped she wasn't making the biggest mistake of her life.

# The Plan Goes Awry

A nd so that's my plan," Noh finished. "I don't one hundred percent know if it will work, but I think it's worth a try." She had just explained to Trina and Caleb DeMarck how they might polarize the machine's flow of energy and create a reverse black hole, forcing everything inside the orb to come out the way it had gone in.

"Let's do it!" Trina said, ready for action as she floated beside Noh. The physics teacher nodded in agreement, even though he hadn't heard Trina's exclamation because she was still invisible to him.

Noh stuck her hand into her pocket and pulled out the evil eye stone. It felt heavier than usual in her hand. She hadn't actually mentioned the evil eye stone when she had explained her plan, figuring the less the physics teacher knew about her ghost-seeing abilities, the better. Now as he watched her expectantly she decided she wasn't quite ready to share her good luck charm with him just yet. She would wait until the last possible second before she would let him see any ghosts.

Happy with her decision, Noh gestured to Caleb DeMarck and he began to set her plan into motion. He took out the two pieces of matching paper, each covered with equations. Next he pulled both sets of wires out of the electrodes and switched them, so that the wires now crossed each other before going back into the base of the machine.

When the physics teacher gave her the thumbs-up, Noh flipped the switch on the machine. Instead of the room getting colder as it had before, it now started to get hotter and hotter until Noh thought she was going to melt.

"I think it's working," Trina said, and Noh could see that the heat was affecting her ghostly friend, too. Ripples of heat poured from Trina's ghostly essence, making Noh feel even hotter. She looked over at Caleb DeMarck and saw him wiping beads of sweat from his forehead. He gave her another thumbs-up.

Suddenly a flash of light filled the room, making Noh's vision swim with color. When she opened her eyes again, she saw the orb floating in the middle of the room, except now it wasn't glowing anymore. Instead it was the color of the midnight sky.

"Trina! You have to guide him out!" Noh screamed over the rush of air that was being expelled out of the orb. She had been right! Reversing the polarity had created an anti–black hole, sending out energy instead of sucking it in.

"Henry!" Trina called, her arms outstretched. "Follow my voice!"

To her surprise, it wasn't Henry who popped out of the orb but her friend Nelly, holding hands with Thomas!

The other ghosts quickly moved to Trina's side.

"Henry's in there too," Nelly said, her voice high and frightened. Trina thought it was the first time she had ever heard fear in Nelly's voice.

"Henry!" Nelly and Trina called together over the rushing air, their voices blending into one.

"There's not much time left!" Noh cried. She could feel the machine starting to tremble beside her. She was afraid that if she didn't pull the switch soon, it might explode.

"Henry!" Nelly and Trina called again, but still he didn't appear.

"Henry!" Noh cried. "Henry! There's no time!"

Noh let go of the switch and started to move toward the orb. Maybe if she could get close enough, she could make Henry hear her. . . .

She felt a strong hand clasp her shoulder, and she turned to see Caleb DeMarck standing beside her.

"I don't see any ghosts yet!" he shouted over the roar of the machine, his eyes dark with frustration.

"My friend needs my help first—," Noh began, but the words caught in her throat when she felt a surge of heat bloom inside her fist that was clutching the evil eye stone. The heat instantly shot up her arm, pooling at the place where the physics teacher's hand was grasping her shoulder. There was another flash of light, this time so bright it made Noh's eyes double blink, but not before she witnessed something shoot out from inside the orb, bypass her, and slam right into the physics teacher's chest, engulfing him in a pale, golden glow that slowly faded away into nothingness. Still gripping

198

Noh's arm, he made a funny, gurgling noise low in his throat and then lurched forward, almost causing her to lose her balance.

"Mr. DeMarck!" Noh cried, steadying herself against the wall. It took all her strength to keep them both from being flung backward by the flow of energy the darkened orb was expelling.

The machine let out a loud hiss, and Noh realized that one of the circuits had blown. Now the machine started to tremble even harder, its metallic body clanging so loudly the sound hurt Noh's ears.

"Who are you?" the physics teacher asked, his voice groggy as if he'd just woken up. Noh looked over at him, surprised at his question, but before she could answer, the physics teacher's eyes popped wide open and he pointed at something behind Noh's head. She followed his gaze to where Trina, Nelly, and Thomas were huddled together by the base of the machine. "Two little girls, a boy in a cap . . . and an orb, pitch-black in color. Am I right?" he asked.

"That's right," Noh said, the heat from the stone coursing up her arm. She realized that she was acting as some kind of human conduit. As long as Caleb DeMarck

was touching her—and through her the evil eye stone—he was able to see the ghosts.

"Are they . . . *real*?" the physics teacher asked, his voice full of amazement.

Noh nodded, but her attention was quickly pulled back to Henry's plight. "We have to help my friend," Noh said, looking over at the trembling machine. Caleb DeMarck nodded at her words.

Noh knew time was of the essence. She had to get Henry out before the machine exploded. She swallowed hard and took a tentative step forward, ready to call Henry's name again, but before she could go farther, she felt the physics teacher's hand grip her shoulder.

"Let *me* try," he said, pulling her back from the orb. "You're too little. You won't be able to get close enough without being blown away. And the way this machine is behaving, we might only have this one chance."

Noh didn't trust the physics teacher one little bit, but what he said made sense. The orb was sending out so much energy that she could barely stand, let alone fight her way inside it.

Without waiting for an answer, Caleb DeMarck released her arm and began to make his way toward the

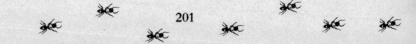

201

pitch-black orb. Then Noh remembered that the physics teacher wouldn't be able to see Henry without the stone. She had to give it to him now before it was too late!

She opened her mouth to yell at him to wait, but a dark and slimy thought twisted around inside her head, making her hesitate. It hissed at her, reminding her that if she gave Caleb DeMarck the stone, she might never get it back from him once he understood its power—and that meant she would turn back into a normal girl again, without the special ability to see her new ghost friends.

With a sinking heart, Noh realized this was the hardest decision she had ever been asked to make: She could either save Henry or keep her ghost sight, but she couldn't do both.

# The Truth Hits Hard

**W**ait!" Noh cried, causing the physics teacher to stop in his tracks.

She took a deep breath and stuffed the evil eye stone into Caleb DeMarck's hand. He seemed surprised as his fingers closed over its warmth.

"Are you sure . . . ?" he asked.

"It's how I can see the ghosts," she said.

The physics teacher instantly understood.

"Thank you, my dear. I wouldn't have stood a chance in there without this."

Noh was surprised by the physics teacher's choice of words. Until now he had never called her "my dear," but before she could linger on what this new twist might mean, the machine gave another horrific shudder.

"Just save my friend Henry, please," Noh said, smiling weakly.

Caleb DeMarck nodded.

"If I get stuck inside and can't get back out, pull the lever before the machine explodes," he said as he turned back toward the orb. "It's the only safe way. Promise?"

"Promise," Noh forced herself to reply. She would say it, but that didn't mean she would do it.

Noh felt empty as she watched him go. She had just given away the one thing that made her special. She wanted to cry, but tears would do nothing to get the evil eye stone back. She only hoped her sacrifice had been made in time to save her ghostly friend.

"Henry, my boy?!" Caleb DeMarck yelled. His voice was louder than hers, loud enough to be heard over the rush of energy from the orb.

Suddenly Noh felt a sharp yank on her arm, like she was being pulled forward. She realized that the heat in her arm wasn't dissipating like she had expected, but instead was only getting hotter. It seemed that the closer Caleb DeMarck got to the orb, the more Noh felt the pull on her arm. It was like she was somehow connected to the evil eye stone by an invisible cord of energy, so that wherever it went, part of her went with it.

Transfixed, Noh watched as Caleb DeMarck took a few more steps, getting as close as possible to the orb without actually going inside it. The force of the energy surrounding the thing was so intense that it almost blew the physics teacher off his feet, but he held his ground.

"Son?!" he called. "Can you hear me?"

Still there was no answer. He reached his hands into the heart of the blackened, swirling energy ball. Noh felt the heat in her arm intensify, making her cringe a little from the pain.

"I think I can see him," the physics teacher called. "I'm going in!"

Before Noh understood what he intended, he had disappeared inside the pulsing orb. As soon as he crossed the threshold Noh's arm began to burn like wildfire, forcing her to grit her jaw against the burning ache. She closed her eyes, hoping to make the pain go away, but instead it only got worse with every passing second.

The machine began to shimmy and shake next to her, but Noh's arm hurt too much for her to take any notice.

"Noh, the machine!" Trina cried. "It's smoking!"

Trina's words caught at the edge of Noh's consciousness, and she looked up to find bright orange flames licking the side of the machine. Distracted from her pain by this new dilemma, her brain spun around like a hamster wheel. She could usually figure anything out if she thought hard enough about it, but this problem only had one very impossible answer.

"Pull the lever, Noh!" Trina yelled, leaving Nelly and Thomas cowering on the floor to float over to where Noh stood. That was the exact impossible answer that Noh had been afraid of.

"I know I promised, but I can't," Noh said angrily, tears pricking her eyes. "If I do, they might never be able to come back again!"

Without realizing it, she had made a decision—and there was no going back. She was Henry's friend, and friends didn't leave each other behind at the first sign of trouble.

"We're staying too, then," Trina said with a nervous smile, and Nelly and Thomas nodded their agreement.

"Friends stick together," Nelly said, her voice barely loud enough for Noh to hear, but it was like getting a shot of feel-good juice. It was hard to believe that she had come to New Newbridge with no friends and in only two days she had made four new wonderful ones. If she hadn't been in such a dire situation, Noh would have said it was the most incredible two days of her entire life.

Right before her eyes, the whole machine was being engulfed in flames. Noh could see them licking around the edges of the machine's metal body. Smoke poured out the top of it, making Noh's eyes water and her throat burn. She tried to cover her face with her shirt to keep the smoke out, but it didn't help one bit.

She thought about her dad and her aunt and how sad they would be when they discovered she'd disappeared. She knew they'd think that she was upset about having to go to New Newbridge and that she had run away to spite them. They would have no way to discover the truth. She doubted anyone else knew about this secret place, so no one would ever think to look for her here. Besides, she'd be a ghost just like Trina and Henry by then, so it wouldn't matter anyway.

Until that moment, Noh had never realized how much she loved her family. Now she felt that love like a fist around her heart, squeezing the muscle so hard her chest ached. Tears pricked her eyes, but she fought against them. If she was going to die and become a ghost, then she was determined not to cry about it: Worse things could and might happen to her than just becoming like her friends.

"Henry!" Trina and Nelly cried in unison, and Noh looked up to find Caleb DeMarck's head re-emerging from within the swirl of the orb.

"Mr. DeMarck!" Noh said as she watched him extricate himself from the pull of the swirling energy, a near comatose Henry in his arms.

Suddenly a loud bell-clang, signaling the ignition of the school's fire alarm, filled the air, and a shower of cold water burst from the sprinklers in the ceiling, instantly putting out the flames that had been threatening to consume the room.

The burning ache in Noh's arm fizzled to a more manageable level, and she sighed with relief, tears of pain and happiness sliding down her already wet cheeks. She ignored the bites on her legs as the ant venom began to make them itch like crazy, everything forgotten in the wake of seeing her ghostly friend in one piece again.

*But wait,* Noh thought as she peered through the

droplets of water cascading from the ceiling, *that can't be right*. There was something strange about Henry. Something she couldn't, at first, put her finger on—and then it dawned on Noh what that something strange was: *Henry wasn't a ghost anymore—he was physically solid!*

Suddenly she understood *exactly* what Eustant P. Druthers had been doing when he had built the mysterious machine: He had been trying to make ghosts real again. Electricity was just the unforeseen by-product of an even more ingenious invention!

With the answer to the machine's true purpose excitedly swimming around in her brain, Noh threw the switch on the machine. Instantly the orb disappeared and Henry became ghostly again, the machine's power no longer exerting a hold over him. He floated down through Caleb DeMarck's solid, living arms just as the machine let out a low growl, spit out a plume of thick gray smoke, and whined to a stop.

As suddenly as the fire alarm had started, it stopped, and the sprinklers slowed down to a trickle. They all stood in silence, waiting for the machine to do something else, but it seemed to be finished. Trina, who was never at a loss for words, spoke first.

"Well, that wasn't *so* bad—," she began brightly, but before she could continue her thought, the lightbulb above their heads unexpectedly fell to the floor and exploded into a million pieces, flooding the room in darkness.

# Scary Trouble

The nasty thing that still refuses to be named had been waiting for a long time. It had tasted something *big* once upon a time, and now it was hungry for more.

It had followed the teacher (and the ants) and the two girls (one alive, one dead) down into the hidden room, but it hadn't shown its hand. It had waited patiently while the machine had tried to suck up the ghost's soul, and it waited even more patiently as the machine—rewired now—had *released* the three other ghost souls it had originally sucked up.

It had waited as the teacher—who wasn't what he appeared to be, the nasty thing knew for a fact—pulled the ghost boy to safety, and it had waited as the lightbulb, the only source of illumination in the room, had shattered into a million pieces on the floor.

Then, with the room in complete darkness, the nasty thing made its move.

# Noh Indigestion

Trina? Is that you?" Noh said, feeling something brush against her shoulder. She whirled around, thrusting her hands out before her, searching for the someone or something that might explain the horrible feeling she was having deep in the pit of her stomach.

It might've been dark in the secret room, but a little darkness had never scared Noh before. What scared Noh now was the terrible sense that something large and scary was trying to swallow her whole. She flung her hands frantically into the air, pushing the bad feeling away, but the more she struggled, the more the feeling took over even more of her body.

She tried to call out for help, but her throat didn't

seem to be working. She wanted to cry, but her tear ducts didn't seem to be working either. She was having trouble breathing, and her body was beginning to feel like it was weighted down with lead.

Then, as quickly as the feeling had overcome her, it got *worse*.

"Help me!" Noh screamed, the darkness increasing her fear. Suddenly she wasn't standing anymore. Instead, she was free-falling through black emptiness, her stomach halfway to her throat, just the way it felt when she was on a roller coaster at the fair. She opened her eyes, but there was only blackness as she continued to fall farther and farther into nothingness.

As she flew through the nothingness Noh had an idea. She reached around in her pocket, her fingers struggling to grasp the smooth surface of the evil eye stone—but then she remembered that it was gone. She had given it to Caleb DeMarck to save Henry.

*Help me,* she thought, wishing as hard as she could on the evil eye stone that was no longer hers. *Somebody help me!*

Then, abruptly, the free-falling stopped and Noh felt herself suspended in the air, floating. She looked around her, but the only thing she could see was a tiny white light shooting toward her. The closer it got, the larger it got until Noh was able to see that it wasn't a light at all . . . *but a boy.*

"Who are you?" Noh asked, even though she didn't need to. She knew exactly who he was.

The boy didn't reply. He just looked at her with his sad blue eyes, then looked down to where he was holding out his hand for her to take. And that's when she noticed it: *four missing fingers displayed for all to see.*

"Hubert?"

The boy looked up at her and grinned, surprised that she knew his name. Noh realized that he looked exactly how she'd imagined he would look: short blond hair; wide, sad blue eyes; and a cute turned-up nose.

"Where are we?" she asked, but Hubert wouldn't or *couldn't* tell her. Instead, he offered her his hand again, and this time she took it. Instantly she felt her body being pulled up, up, up, and away from the darkness.

As she let the ghost boy guide her toward what she hoped was safety Noh realized something important—something that made her heart sing with joy: She could see Hubert—and she didn't need the evil eye stone's help to do it!

# Why Ants Aren't King

Trina and Nelly saw the nasty thing attack Noh. Thomas, scared completely out of his wits, covered his eyes with his cap. Henry was still out like a light, but neither of the girls would have expected him to be of much help even if he *had* been awake.

The nasty thing was huge—the size of a small elephant, with large saber-tooth tiger teeth and great big furry arms that had wrapped themselves around its unsuspecting victim. Unlike Noh and the physics teacher, Trina and Nelly didn't need the lightbulb hanging from the ceiling to see what was going on around them, but they were both so shocked by the sight of the nasty thing trying to eat their friend that it took them a moment to understand what needed doing.

"Something's attacking Noh," Trina cried, but just as the words left her mouth, the nasty thing swallowed Noh whole. "Oh no, it just ate her!"

The nasty thing, its face a corpulent mass of squirming darkness, turned toward Trina and smiled horribly at her, revealing sharp gray teeth and a slavering red tongue.

"The ants!" Nelly said, her voice full of authority. "They can help us."

Trina raced over to the physics teacher and tried to shake him into action, but her ghostly hands slid right through his shoulders.

"How do you make the ants work?" she almost screamed. The nasty thing was slowly moving toward them, its tongue lolling out of its mouth like a big red slug. It watched them with a nasty look on its face, like it wanted to eat all of them whole too.

"I don't know what you mean," the physics teacher said, looking truly mystified by her question.

"Your pockets," Trina yelled. "It's in your pockets! Please, hurry!"

Caleb DeMarck wrinkled his brow, uncertainty flooding his face, but he did as Trina asked, sinking his hands into his pockets.

"My goodness," he said, "you were right!" He held up a handful of the fluffy white stuff, a big smile transforming his face. "Tell me what to do, because I can't see a thing!" he said, getting into the swing of things.

"The monster's at two o'clock," Nelly cried. "Throw it there!"

The physics teacher let loose with the white stuff. It landed almost at the nasty thing's feet. The ants went crazy, squirming all over one another to get to the stuff first, but they didn't stop there. They instantly sensed that there was more for them to feast on than just concentrated aphid milk. They began to climb up the nasty thing, covering it with bites as they tried to make it their evening snack.

The nasty thing let out a gargantuan roar and began to swing its body back and forth like a dog trying to shake the water out of its fur after a bath. It stamped its feet like thunder as it reeled around the room, its steps grinding into the floor and shaking the whole place like an earthquake.

"It's working!" Trina cried, dizzy with happiness, but the happiness didn't last very long.

The ant bites might have made a human girl like

Noh itch with pain, but the nasty thing was anything but a human girl. It continued to hold Noh captive inside its big belly while the ants swarmed all over its furry body, biting away with every ounce of energy they had inside them.

"Noh!" Trina screamed, fear for her friend's safety making her ghostly form shimmer in the darkness.

But it was too late. The ants had failed, and now her friend Noh was going to be the nasty thing's lunch.

# Hubert Was Here

Noh opened her eyes to find herself sitting in a familiar place: the special spot by the lake Hullie had shown her earlier in the afternoon. Of course, now that the light had fled for the day and evening was upon them, the woods seemed a whole lot more ominous than they had back then.

The place gave Noh an icky feeling down in the pit of her stomach, but she tried to ignore it so she could focus on more important things.

*Like getting back into her body.*

She had realized her precarious position almost immediately. Hubert might've saved her spirit, but he'd left her body to molder away inside the monster that had swallowed her. Now all she could do was watch as the wind danced through the canopy of trees above her, scattering a few errant leaves to the ground. It was very disheartening to see the wind blowing around you but not be able to feel it. It made Noh's heart sting to think about never hugging her dad or eating a bowl of yummy tomato soup again.

"You don't like it here?" Noh heard Hubert say, and she turned at the sound of his voice to find him sitting in the grass across from her, picking at the clover, head lowered so she couldn't see his eyes.

"I don't *not* like it," Noh offered. It was the best she could do. If she said anything of a more positive nature, it would be a lie, and she did *not* want to be a liar. To keep herself safe, she decided to change the subject instead. "Why are we here?"

Hubert shrugged. "I dunno. I like it here, and it's safe from prying eyes."

Noh had to agree with him. It *was* safe from prying eyes, but only because it was so creepy at night that she couldn't imagine anyone else wanting to bother with it.

"I appreciate you helping me," Noh continued, "but I really need to get back to my friends before they start worrying about me."

Hubert looked up at her now, his eyes shining, and Noh thought he looked like the saddest boy she had ever seen.

"You don't want to stay here with me?" he asked, wrinkling his brow.

Noh shook her head. "I'm not a ghost yet, so I don't think I'm really allowed."

"But if I don't take you back, then the whatsit will finish eating you, and then you can stay with me forever," Hubert said plainly. "You can be my friend."

Noh realized that if she didn't step in and take charge right then, Hubert might make the choice for her, sealing her fate forever. She could see he was a very lonely ghost, but she didn't think sacrificing herself to make him happy was a smart decision. She knew from experience that the only person you could ever make happy was yourself.

"What if I promise to come visit you every week while I'm here at New Newbridge?" Noh offered. "I could be your alive friend—and that's way better than being a ghost friend."

She could see Hubert thinking about her suggestion, weighing it in his mind.

"Why is it better?"

Noh had her answer down pat.

"It's better because an alive friend can go anywhere and do anything. They aren't stuck in one place like ghosts are. I can be your spy and tell you about all the things that are happening in the world outside of New Newbridge Academy."

Instantly Hubert's face lit up, and he grinned at her.

"You'd do that? You'd be my secret spy?"

Noh nodded.

"And you wouldn't tell anyone about me," Hubert added, the light in his eyes fading a bit as he spoke.

"Not if you don't want me to," Noh agreed, "but I know for a fact that there are a lot of other ghosts at New Newbridge who would love to meet you."

Hubert shook his head vigorously. "Only you know about me, and I want to keep it that way," he said.

Noh didn't argue with him. If he wanted to keep himself hidden away out here by the lake, she wasn't going to rat him out.

"Okay, it's a deal then," Noh said, holding out her hand for Hubert to shake. He reached out to grasp her fingers, but as soon as they touched, she felt a funny prickling sensation all over her body like she'd been plunged into a freezing cold shower.

"Don't forget your promise," Hubert said softly.

And then Noh disappeared.

# The Evil Eye Stone

It was still black as night inside the hidden room, so the physics teacher, who couldn't see in the dark, didn't know that the ants had not succeeded. Instead, the man who had once been Caleb DeMarck—but was now someone else entirely—was much more interested in the hot, uncomfortable sensation he was feeling in his right hand—the one that was still clutching the girl's magic stone!

He knew exactly what the stone was and what it wanted from him—and that was because he had helped to create the stone in the first place!

*Release me!* the stone sang in his head. *Let me fly and save the girl! The ants have failed!*

"Of course, my friend," the man who had once been

Caleb DeMarck whispered to the stone. "But first, I want to see the beast in its true form."

It only took the stone a moment to understand what the man wanted, but when it did the darkness immediately lifted away from the former physics teacher's eyes like a curtain, and he could see the nasty thing in all its glory.

He had never seen anything as strange or ugly as the monster standing in front of him, and he almost yelped in fear. The nasty thing caught him staring, and it hissed at him like an angry house cat.

The nasty thing, which was really nothing more than an accumulation of all the fears of all the children who had ever attended New Newbridge Academy, had spent its whole life hiding away from prying eyes, lingering on the edges of where the living world and the dead world connected, and it was wholly unprepared for the fear it felt at being seen by a real live grown-up human being.

The evil eye stone sensed the nasty thing's terror and began to grow even hotter. The former Caleb DeMarck let the stone sizzle in his hand, the pain a reminder that he was human again after all these years.

*Throw me!* the stone cried in his head. *Let me fly! Let me save my new friend!*

This time, the words were like a magic spell. They weaved themselves inside the former physics teacher's brain, and with a twinkle in his eye, he wound up his arm, took a step forward, and threw the most perfect fastball the world would never see, shooting the evil eye stone right into the nasty thing's mouth.

The nasty thing yowled with anger and pain as the evil eye stone burned the insides of its gullet. When the stone reached the nasty thing's stomach, it made a loud popping sound and the nasty thing howled in frustration. Eating something big wasn't supposed to be *this* much trouble!

The nasty thing unhappily realized that it was no match for a magical stone that so badly wanted to be back with its mistress. It let go of its hold on Noh, and with its tail between its legs, it scurried out of the hidden room as fast as it could go, shrinking itself to the size of a flea as it made its way out of the building.

Noh blinked, surprised to find herself standing in the middle of the hidden room, holding the evil eye stone tightly in her hand. In the darkness she reached out for Hubert, but she couldn't find him anywhere.

"Hubert?" Noh said weakly, but there was no answer. *Her savior was gone.*

"Where did Hubert go . . . ?" she started to say, but then words failed her. The weight of all the crazy things that had happened to Noh since she'd arrived at New Newbridge began to sink in, and she fainted dead away just as a loud banging sound trickled down through the ceiling.

With a discreet *click*, the secret doorway opened to reveal first Hullie, whose bushy hair shone like a halo around his head, and then a tidy young woman who could only be Noh's aunt Sarah, peering into the secret room with only a flashlight to illuminate the darkness.

"Thank goodness I replaced those old sprinkler heads when I did," Hullie said as he shone the beam of his flashlight down onto the charred wreckage of the machine. "It could've gotten pretty hot down here, otherwise."

He moved the light away from the machine, letting it slide across the floor and over to the spot where Noh's unconscious form lay. The man who had once been Caleb DeMarck was kneeling on the ground beside her, looking very worried.

Following the beam of the flashlight, Aunt Sarah scampered into the secret room and crouched down beside her unconscious niece. Hullie was fast on her heels, pulling a brand-spanking-new lightbulb from his pocket at the same time.

"Thank you so much for looking after her, Caleb," Aunt Sarah said, smiling up at the former Caleb DeMarck. She might've acted differently had she known the man before her wasn't the *real* physics teacher anymore, but she didn't, so gratitude was all he got.

"She was very brave," the former physics teacher managed to say before looking down at his hands so no one would see the scarlet blush creeping up his cheeks.

Luckily, Aunt Sarah didn't notice his embarrassment because she was too involved in her own thoughts.

"Oh, Hullie, I know it's important to let her find her own way, but what if something truly terrible had happened," she said, her voice thick with worry.

Hullie finished putting the new bulb in place, then turned the light back on, letting a warm glow expose the mess that was once the secret room.

"You know the rules, Sarah," he said, popping a fresh toothpick into his mouth as he moved to stand beside

231

her, placing a reassuring arm on her shoulder. "No interference, unless it's specifically asked for."

Aunt Sarah nodded, but it was apparent she didn't wholly agree with his words.

"Besides," Hullie added, giving her a wink, "that's why I keep both my eyes wide open. So creatures like that old *nasty thing* don't get too out of hand at New Newbridge Academy."

And with that, Hullie reached down and picked Noh up, lifting her over his shoulder as if she was the lightest thing in the world.

"Let's get this girl cleaned up and off to bed before she catches cold," he continued, making his way back to the secret door with Aunt Sarah right behind him.

Trina and Nelly watched silently as the procession of realies left the room. To their surprise, (the former) Caleb DeMarck stopped in the doorway and gave them a small wave good-bye. He couldn't see them anymore, but somehow it didn't matter. In his heart he knew they were there, waving good-bye to him in return.

# It's All in the Soup

**N**oh sat up in bed with a tray of tomato soup and grilled cheese sandwich squares resting gently on her lap. The tomato soup was better than amazing, Noh decided as she took another spoonful. It had just the right amount of cream in it so that it wasn't too tomatoey. She picked up one of the grilled cheese squares—it was made with a hefty amount of American cheese and toasted white bread, no crusts—and took a gigantic bite.

"Yummy," Noh said to herself after she'd swallowed the bite.

There was a knock on her

door, and Noh sat up straighter, almost spilling her soup.

"Come in!" she called, but just exerting that amount of energy wiped her out. Whatever nasty creature had attacked her, it had succeeded in stealing a good chunk of her energy. She figured she was gonna need at least two weeks—and lots of good, hearty food—to recuperate, and by then summer would almost be over. Just a few more weeks and she'd be in the library studying for tests, not chasing after secret papers and solving mysterious occurrences . . . and nearly getting eaten by hungry monsters.

Of course, everyone *else* believed that there'd been a freak electrical fire down in the basement and that, luckily, the physics teacher had been passing by and had smelled the smoke and rushed in to save her.

Noh figured maybe that was for the best. She didn't want to frighten anyone by letting out the fact that monsters and ghosts existed at New Newbridge—at least until she could figure out what to do about the monster part.

The door opened and her aunt Sarah, followed by a sheepish-looking Caleb DeMarck, came into the room.

"I hope you don't mind company, but Mr. DeMarck

wanted to say good-bye before he left," her aunt said as she pulled the chair out from underneath Noh's desk and moved it closer to the bed.

"Good-bye?" Noh said, looking up at the physics teacher, who indeed was wearing a traveling coat and a gray fedora. He also had a large briefcase under his arm, which he set on the floor beside the chair before sitting down. It had been almost twenty-four hours since the attack—most of which Noh had spent in a dark and dreamless sleep that the town physician said was likely due to the shock she had suffered from so many ant bites—but Caleb DeMarck looked like a different person.

Gone was the know-it-all boy, and in his place was what seemed like a wiser, more thoughtful man. Noh watched as her aunt Sarah gently shut the door on her way out, giving them a bit of privacy.

"Yes, I'm afraid that I have to go away on a very important mission," he said, taking off his hat and placing it in his lap so he could play with its brim as he spoke. "But I wanted to share something with you before I left."

Noh nodded.

"You see, I am not who I appear to be," he began.

This made Noh sit up straighter in her bed, the soup almost spilling into her lap.

"When you reversed the polarity on the Matter Re-Former—"

"Is that what the machine's called?" Noh asked, curiosity getting the better of her.

He nodded. "Yes, that is its given name. Sadly, I cannot take credit for its name *or* its design because I am not the machine's inventor," he continued. "That title belongs to my mentor, Professor Eustant P. Druthers."

It only took Noh a moment to remember where she had heard that name before.

"Wasn't he the man who built this school?" she said, her brain sizzling with this new piece of information.

The former physics teacher nodded.

"So, if you're not Caleb DeMarck, then who are you?" Noh asked, this time actually knocking some of her soup onto the bedcover in her excitement.

The man looked down at his hands as if he were deciding how much information to divulge. Finally, having made his decision, he looked back up at Noh and smiled. "On pain of death you must never tell anyone what I am about to tell you," he said.

Noh nodded so hard it hurt. "I promise."

The former physics teacher nervously scratched his chin and then began. "My real name is Karl Freund. I was once a student here at the New Newbridge Academy, but when Professor Druthers realized my talent for inventing, he took me on as one of his five assistants."

"Wow!" Noh said, loving Karl Freund's story immediately.

"Yes," he said, becoming bashful, "it was amazing for me. All the incredible inventions I imagined in my brain were given life under Professor Druthers's tutelage. I spent years honing my talent for scientific invention under his watchful eye while we built many machines together, and I even had a hand in the creation of the Power Magnifier you carry with you—"

"The Power Magnifier?" Noh repeated. "Wait, do you mean my evil eye stone?"

Karl Freund nodded, pleased she had made the connection so quickly. "The Power Magnifier takes on whatever special power it is exposed to, magnifying it a hundredfold. It is a very useful tool," Karl added, "so long as it does not fall into the wrong hands."

His words made Noh shiver.

"It bestows the last power it has magnified on the next person who possesses it—even those who would use it for evil."

Noh swallowed hard.

"Yes, my dear, it is *you* who are gifted with the ability to see and interact with the dead—and the stone only magnified your power," Karl said gravely. "I was able to view your ghostly friends while I held the stone, and so now I, too, know your secret. You must be very careful with whom you share this information. There are many, like the dastardly Caleb DeMarck, who would steal your gift and use it to further their own means."

"He *was* pretty dastardly, wasn't he?" Noh whispered.

"Yes, he is," Karl agreed.

"Wait, you just used the present tense," Noh wondered out loud. No sooner had the words flown from her lips than she realized what this might mean: Caleb DeMarck was still here among them!

"I know what I am about to tell you will seem highly improbable, but it is the truth," Karl Freund said.

"After all the strange things I've seen over the past few days, I'd pretty much believe anything," Noh said.

This seemed to give Karl Freund more confidence.

"Caleb DeMarck and I share the same body—"

"Wow," was all Noh could manage.

"Even now he seethes because he is trapped in here with me and cannot steal the Power Magnifier," Karl Freund added. "For now, I can control him, but not forever. That is why I must go and find one of Professor Druthers's other assistants—wherever they may be after all these years—so that I might be cured of this strange and unsettling dilemma."

His story finished, Karl Freund got up and put his fedora back on his head.

"Well, at least we are safe from Mr. DeMarck for now—and I am very pleased that you are feeling better," he continued. He tipped his hat and moved toward the door. "You gave your poor aunt a horrible scare. I am afraid she will be watching you like a hawk for a long while to come," he added, his hand on the doorknob.

"Wait!" Noh cried, stopping him. "You never said how you got in the machine in the first place."

Karl Freund gave her a pleased grin as he stepped away from the door. "A freak accident. We were testing the Matter Re-Former and something went wrong. I was sucked into the machine and remained there, frozen in time, until you rescued me from my prison. Upon my release, my spirit attached itself to the first body it came in contact with: your physics teacher."

As crazy as the whole thing might sound to someone else, it made perfect sense to Noh.

"But how come no one ever tried to get you back?" Noh asked, concerned.

Karl Freund shook his head sadly. "That I do not know—"

"But how long were you trapped in the machine?" Noh interrupted, trying to get all the facts.

Karl Freund thought about this question for a moment before answering. "The year was 1951 . . . and I was seventeen."

Noh quickly did the math in her head, the number causing her to cringe inside.

"It was a very long time to be left alone. And I hope, in my travels, to discover why it was so," Karl Freund said as he picked up his briefcase again and returned to the door. He stopped in the doorway and turned back around, pulling a folder from the briefcase and handing it to Noh.

"Until we meet again, Noleen Maypother."

Then he tipped his hat to Noh one final time, opened the door, and was gone.

"He's like a different person," her aunt Sarah said as she came back into the room, marveling at the change in her coworker. "I bet you didn't know that Mr. DeMarck and I went to school together—"

Noh almost toppled her tray onto the floor.

"*You* went to New Newbridge?" she said, staring at her aunt.

"Of course I did," her aunt said. "On scholarship, mind you."

"No one ever told me that," Noh said. She couldn't believe that she hadn't known her aunt had gone to school here. It was weird, like finding out that your parents weren't your parents, or something.

"New Newbridge has always had a place in its heart for *special* children," her aunt began. "In fact, it seems to call to them, inviting them to learn and explore their talents here."

"What do you mean by the word 'special'?" Noh asked curiously.

"I think you know exactly what I mean, Noh.

You're a scholarship student like I was," her aunt said mysteriously. "That means New Newbridge called you here—and it's why the evil eye stone found you. Special things are attracted to special people."

Noh asked her aunt Sarah to explain more, but her aunt shook her head.

"You need to rest now. I'll be back later to check on you." That was all her aunt would say. Noh nodded, closing her eyes to show that she wanted to get some rest too. Her aunt gave her a kiss on the forehead and gently shut the door behind her on the way out.

Noh waited until she couldn't hear her aunt's foot-steps in the hall anymore, and then she opened her eyes and slid open the folder that Karl Freund had given her.

"What's that?" Trina said, popping up beside the bed, her riding helmet askew on her head. She'd been in the middle of refereeing a chess game between Henry and Thomas when she had remembered that she'd promised to check on Noh.

"Look," Noh said as she held up the two secret lemon-inked papers covered in spidery equations.

"I wonder how many other secret papers are hidden in the school," Trina said.

Noh shrugged, her eyes finding the evil eye stone where it was sitting in a place of honor on her dresser top. Just knowing the stone was nearby made her feel stronger and braver . . . ready to take on as many mysteries as the world saw fit to throw her way. The evil eye stone wasn't the key to Noh's ghost sight, it only enhanced it.

"I know another secret place," Trina offered. "Behind the mirrors in the girls' bathroom. I bet there's lots of cool stuff there."

"Yeah?" Noh said, thinking about her toothbrush that got stuck in the bathroom mirror.

"It's pretty neat," Trina said. "I can show you, if you want."

Noh didn't have to think twice about her answer.

"Count me in, but first, let's find the nasty thing that tried to eat me," she said. "The other students will be coming back to New Newbridge really soon, and we can't let it hurt anyone else!"

"Deal!" Trina said, excited by the idea of another adventure coming so soon after their first. Without thinking, she held up her pinkie so they could pinkie swear and seal the deal, but it wasn't until Noh grinned sheepishly at her that Trina remembered her friend was a realie—and realies and ghosts couldn't touch.

"Deal," Noh replied instead. And then the two girls—one a ghost and the other living—hunkered down and began to make their plans.